# COMMAND AND CONTROL
# HEAVY HOOK

## JAMES D. MITCHELL

BERKLEY BOOKS, NEW YORK

*Dedication*

This book is dedicated to my son, Brandon J. Mitchell (Feb. 5, 1964–Mar. 5, 1964). And, to the children of the Hmong tribesmen of Northeastern Laos—their faith and courage in the wake of war's cruelty will always be remembered by myself and others who came to know and love them.

*Acknowledgments*

Grateful acknowledgment is conveyed to Sam and Bac Eaton, Richard Lay, Jim Morris, Jeff Hardwick, and Amelia. Additional thanks to the Peter Miller Agency, NYC.

COMMAND AND CONTROL: HEAVY HOOK

A Berkley Book/published by arrangement with
the author

PRINTING HISTORY
Berkley edition/June 1991

ISBN: 0-425-12728-1

# CHARLIE'S CLOSE CALL . . .

There was no mistaking what he was smoking—I'd smelled it many times—Ruby Queen always stunk like a burning rattail.

"Kinda laid back this morning aren't you, Punky?" I whispered under my breath, keeping my rifle muzzle aimed at his slouched torso.

Soon, several other motley-garbed Pats ambled down the trail with all the enthusiasm of a Mississippi road gang. Four men total.

I squinted at the trail surface trying to see if our boot cleats had left any tracks. The matted, leafy surface told me that tracks were unlikely but I couldn't be sure.

The men talked for a moment then continued on. They were obviously feeling no inhibition about danger. They were so close I could nail them all with one burst . . .

# Chapter 1

The sweet stink of opium washed over me like a hazy net as I entered the dim, bamboo hooch. My eyes stung from the thick fog of smoke. Restraining an urge to cough, I eased my CAR-15 sling over my neck and leaned the rifle against a thatched wall. I turned, made a quick praying gesture, and darted a respectful nod to the five elder Hmong tribesmen squatted in a half-circle around a boy lying in the center of the hut.

The old men smiled through black, stained teeth and returned my silent greeting—they all radiated that glazed opium grin. I squinted and knelt near the boy to inspect the wounds. Using my bush hat, I fanned it over him to clear away the droning mass of flies. His right arm lay limp, loosely attached to a hand hanging by strings of black, rotted flesh. Lumps of crusted blood caked over the remnants of shattered bone protruding through the puffy, swollen forearm. One large chunk of muscle near the elbow had been torn away, severing tendons and exposing more splintered bone. The near-gagging odor of gangrene mingled with the exhaled stream of opium smoke, which the elders kept blowing into the youth's face.

Note: The Hmong tribe of Northern Laos are derogatorily called the "Meo," meaning "barbarian" in Chinese. The term "Meo" *will not* appear in this story.

1

I dramatized an optimistic wink and smiled at the young boy. "You brave Hmong. We go outside. Okay?" I said, touching his warm forehead with the backside of my hand. He tried to return a smile. He was maybe twelve years old.

I leaned toward the door and shouted. "Tuong, *lai day*!"

Tuong, the youngest of my four Montagnard teammates, crawled hurriedly through the entrance and knelt near me. "Rogee, Sar Brett. What you tink? Maybe him be okay?"

Pulling a roach from a mass of dark, yellow pus I replied, "He's going to die unless that arm is amputated right away."

"What do ampoo—"

"It means cut off the arm. Now help me get him out of this opium den."

Suddenly a loud chorus of chants and moans emitted from the old men. They waved their arms upward, stirring the hazy cloud of smoke while they groaned.

Ignoring the prayer ritual I motioned for Tuong to grab the forward sides of the straw mat the boy was lying on while I gripped the other end. As we carefully lifted the makeshift litter, one elder shouted something at Tuong.

"Sar Brett, I tink him say wait for more prayer."

"Fuck more prayer! Tell him what I need right now is more light!"

Tuong grinned, then muttered what sounded like a less profane interpretation of my words. We crouched and exited the hooch with the youngster.

I was fortunate to have Tuong providing interpretation for me. Although he was from the Jeh tribe of Dega in South Vietnam, he'd worked in this area as an observer for the CIA for a year prior to volunteering for CCN recon. He knew the area and was familiar with the Hmong dialect.

Less than twenty minutes before, we'd entered the small Hmong village located west of Na Dao, Laos. I learned immediately from the boy's mother that her son had tripped an NVA booby-trap just yesterday. His mother had led me to the Shaman prayer hut and asked me to help her son because she was forbidden inside the hooch.

I wasn't sure I could save him, but I knew he didn't stand a cricket's chance on a New York sidewalk unless I amputated the infested arm.

Outside, we moved the boy to the cool, shady side of the hooch while motioning the crowd of women, children, and barking dogs away. After placing him on a loose pile of leaves and branches, I dug through my aid pouch and pulled out a Syrette of morphine.

"Tuong," I said, cracking the plastic cover off the needle with my teeth and spitting it away. "Go tell Binkowski to get up here now. *Dee!*"

I'd positioned Ski, Phan, Lok, and Rham near the entrance to the village to maintain a lookout for NVA patrols. I turned my attention to the little boy again and showed him the needle. "This is number-one for you, amigo." I quickly jabbed the small needle into his deltoid and squeezed the tube. The boy didn't flinch.

Looking up, I saw his mother kneeling at her son's head whispering close to his ear as she stroked his hair.

*"Ten anh?"* I asked her, hoping she understood some Vietnamese. The Hmong had dozens of tribes and respective dialects throughout Southeast Asia—I'd learned during my first tour in Nam that the best way to communicate with them was by finding commonly used bits of English, French, or Vietnamese. If that failed I resorted to a mixed bag of facial expressions, sketches drawn in the dirt, and hand and arm signals.

*"Ten ahn?"* I repeated.

The blank look on her face indicated she didn't understand my question.

"Name," I said tapping my chest. "Me name, Yancy. Him name?" I finished, pointing to her son.

"Chung . . . Chung," she answered through a weary smile.

I pulled the cravat from my neck and began wrapping the infected arm below the elbow. Taking a canteen from my web gear, I poured water over the cravat wrap, then gestured to the boy with the open end of the canteen. "Chung, *nuoc*?"

His lethargic nod told me the morphine was taking over. He tried to prop upward on his left elbow. I held the canteen to his lips and gently gripped his nape while he sipped.

"What's up, partner?" Ski shouted through labored breaths as he and Tuong hurried toward me. "What's wrong with him?"

"He triggered an NVA booby-trap. What's the trail status down there?" I questioned, while keeping the canteen held to Chung's lips.

Binkowski dropped to one knee beside me and leaned against his rifle. "We ain't seen nothing yet, partner. I put Rham fifty meters down that steep section of trail that hooks south. Have you noticed there's only women, kids, and old men in this village? Seems weird."

"It's a way of life, buddy. The communists roll into these villages and take all the young men for Uncle Ho's cause. The ones that don't escape or cooperate are shot on the spot. It's called recoil recruitment, but some do escape to join Vang Pao."

"Who's he?"

"He's a Hmong general with the Laotian Army. He's trying to rally and train tribesmen in this region to resist the NVA and Pathet-Lao."

I glanced at Tuong. "Tell mamasan here that I need her to build a fire and heat *beaucoup nuoc*."

"Wha . . . what are you going to do, Brett?" Ski asked.

I withdrew the canteen and leveled a stare into Ski's eyes. "Do you know anything about amputation procedure?"

Ski jerked back like I'd slapped him. "Me? Shi . . .

shit, I can't even spell amputation. But, hey, I saw a movie
once and they—''

''Forget it. How many Syrettes of morphine do you
have?''

''Three, just like you told me to always—''

''Give me those and your knife.''

''Hey, what's wrong with you using your knife?'' he
protested while digging into his small aid pouch.

''Arnold, don't argue. I'm going to need to keep one
hot while I'm cutting with the other one.''

As Tuong and Chung's mother began the fire, I pulled
the cravat downward from the shredded bone and crusted,
blackened flesh around the elbow and took a closer look
at the area near the joint. A thick glob of pus clung to the
scarf as I removed the cloth.

Ski stood abruptly. ''Ah, ah, Brett . . . I better get back.
I mean surely you don't need me for this. Do you?''

''Negative. You make a quick area recon of the northeast side of this hill and find a good rally point and escape
route just in case we get hit. Let me know what you find,
then tell the Cowboys where to assemble if the shit hits
the fan and we get routed. Roger?''

''Roger, Brett,'' he muttered, walking away. He quickly
turned. ''Do you know anything about amputation?''

''I can spell it, Arnold. Move out!''

My roommate at Fort Bragg had been a Special Forces
medic. Once, over a few beers at the club, he'd told me
about amputating a dog's leg during a phase of his medical
training. Now I was digging back through my hazy mem-
ory trying to remember everything he'd said.

Tuong nudged me. ''Sar Brett, maybe trouble come,''
he said, looking beyond me.

I turned to see the Shaman and the elders emerging
from the hut. They walked slowly toward me, formed a
half-circle, and squatted in the bright noonday sun about
ten meters away. The Shaman rested his extended arms

over his knees and stared at the two survival knives I'd placed at the edge of the fire pit.

Raising his arms, he pointed skyward while muttering an emphatic lecture directed mostly at Tuong and Chung's mother. She cast them a bewildered, pleaful look, then glanced at me and bowed her head.

Tuong moved closer to me as the Shaman continued his excited finger-pointing spiel. "Sar Brett, him say you can no take away par of man body. Him say spirits no smile and no happy if man no full when man die."

Tuong's brief description of the situation didn't surprise me. I was aware of the Hmong religious customs. I didn't want to incite a low-level pissing contest with the Shaman—he was following the beliefs that had been passed down through centuries of Hmong Animism. They believed that when a man died, all his parts needed to be intact or the gods wouldn't let him into the heavenly hooch.

But I also knew that the Shaman had a position of authority to uphold in order to save face. If he failed to assert his convictions to the ways of custom he could slip or be pushed off his pedestal.

I placed my rifle on the other side of Chung's litter and stood. I wanted the elders to clearly see that I wasn't about to impose gun-muzzle dogma in order to get my way. I bowed to them, then reached and pulled a small branch from beneath the bed of leaves.

"Follow me, babysan," I said, taking a deep breath. We moved slowly toward the elders.

I knelt and faced the skinny, bare-chested Shaman. Using the branch I drew the figure of a tree in the loose dirt, then looked into the wrinkled face of the village priest.

"Tuong," I said softly, "I want you to tell this man that I understand and respect what the gods, the spirits, tell him. Say that exactly and don't add anything."

Tuong bowed and squatted near the Shaman and me. "Rogee, Sar Brett," he replied darting a dubious look at me before addressing the Shaman.

He conveyed my message to the priest slowly and with a respectful tone. The elders all smiled and mumbled among themselves while nodding their approval.

"Dae like dat you understan, Sar Brett."

"Good," I said, staring conspicuously at the cut end of the branch in my hand. "Now, tell him that the tree from where this branch was cut will grow a new branch if the gods want it to grow a new branch. The gods decide what will grow and what will not grow."

Tuong hesitated for a moment, then pointed at the cut end of the branch and began speaking. When he finished, the Shaman drew a calloused hand to his gray-bearded chin and nodded thoughtfully without reply.

I glanced at Tuong and narrowed my eyes. "Now tell him that Chung, a brave Hmong, is going to die if I do not cut the rotten branch from the tree of his body. Tell him the gods need for him to decide if the boy will live or die. It's up to him."

"Sar Brett," Tuong whispered. "How you know if—"

"Trust me, babysan. Tell him like I said."

Pointing at the branch with one hand, and my training aid sketch with the other, Tuong went about the explanation with the grace and tone of a luxury car salesman opening the door to a new Cadillac. I kept my best poker face focused on the Shaman as Tuong spoke.

When Tuong finished delivering my sales pitch, I handed the small branch to the elder priest, clasped my hands into praying position, and nodded.

The old man studied the severed end of the stick, then embraced it and slowly tilted his head skyward.

"You did good, babysan. Now let's give these gents a minute to think about this." I stood, bowed, and returned to Chung and his mother. I wasn't about to let the little boy simply rot and die if I could help it, but I learned that discretion is sometimes truly the greater part of valor—and it can sure save wear and tear on a man's knuckles in the wrong situation.

# Chapter 2

Chung's mother squatted near her son, fanning him with a large leaf while we waited and watched the village board of directors begin a yakking session. The conference would ultimately decide the life or death of one little boy in a mountainous patch of Laotian jungle. The elders were taking their time and patience was not one of my virtues.

I sat quietly studying the red glow radiating from the knife blades near the fire. I thought back to the agonizing moments when I had to sit and watch my son slowly die of spinal meningitis. I'd married the girl I got pregnant in my senior year at high school. Seven months later she bore us a baby boy. Twenty-nine days into his infancy I went to his crib for his morning feeding and found him near death, his tiny body tinted a hideous blue.

A few hours after rushing him to the hospital we were told that he could not be saved. They said it was best, considering the pain and brain damage he'd suffered, to discontinue life support. I said no. I gave prayer everything I had for three hours while I leaned against the glass ICU housing covering my son—crying, begging God to give him another chance. Finally, I relented.

"Sar Brett. Sar Brett, Ski come," Tuong said, leaning near me and pointing toward the tree line that skirted the northeast side of the village.

Ski plodded toward me with a dramatic look of accomplishment glossing his face. "There's a burned-out area just beyond those trees, Brett. Thirty meters east of that is a big wood pile that'll make a good first rally point, I think. What do you think?"

"Sounds good, partner. Get on back to the team and make sure they know how to find it."

"Roger," he said, looking down at Chung. "I—I thought you were going to amputate, operate on him. What's the holdup?"

I peered toward the elders. "The fucking holdup is that long-winded staff meeting over there."

"Yeah, I see what you mean," he replied, taking a step back and pushing the bush hat up off his brow. "Brett, could—could I talk to you a minute? You know, kinda in private."

"Be right back, Tuong. Watch them," I said, nodding toward the gathering of old men.

A few steps later Binkowski and I stopped and were immediately surrounded by a group of chattering kids.

"Brett, do you remember the first time you chewed me out when I first came on the team? You remember, I—I was supposed to be drawing ammo for the team and I kinda got off—off the subject a little and stopped by the club to visit and have a beer and you—"

"I remember. What's the point here?"

"Ah, well . . . that was the first time but it wasn't the only time you jumped in my shit, and of course I probably deserved it, but you were always—"

"Arnold, will you get to the fucking point!"

"Yes sir, I mean roger, partner. Well, the point is, you reminded me that I needed to keep my mind on the mission. And, well . . ." he continued, while looking down at the children and avoiding my eyes. "Well, I—I kinda think we're getting off the track, the mission here, that's all.

"I mean, we're sitting ducks here in this village and

we're supposed to be looking for that IVS guy. The only reason we risked coming in here was to see if they had seen or knew where Duell was. That's what you told me and now—''

''Hold it, Ski,'' I said, trying to keep the fuse on my temper unignited. ''That little boy over there will be dead in less than two days if I don't stop that gangrene. That means doing something I've never done before. Shit, I'm not a doctor, I'm not even a medic . . . I'd give my R and R for a Special Forces medic right now!

''Anyhow, I'm giving this my best shot, so try and understand that every now and then priorities change. It's the right thing to do. Roger that?''

''Okay, roger.'' Ski answered in a half-hearted tone.

I took a step closer to him and narrowed my eyes. ''How many missions you got under your belt?''

''You know darn well—''

''How many?''

''Two, that's all!''

''That's right, two. And suddenly you're fucking telling me how to drive this RT.'' I caught a glimpse of the children moving away from me.

I lowered my voice. ''I've got sixteen trips across the fence, amigo, and I didn't get through them by not knowing what I'm doing. Your mission right now, buck-sergeant, is to get back and tell the team about that rally point. Move out.''

''Roger,'' he mumbled shyly. ''Sorry, guess I was a little off base. I do trust your—your judgment, Brett. I wasn't meaning to—''

I tapped his shoulder, stirring a small cloud of dust from his fatigues. ''You aren't off base, partner. Just remember it's not always Queensbury rules out here. War is one thing, but if we don't show the people we're fighting for that we care about them, then what the fuck do we hope to win? Understand?'' I cracked a half-grin.

Ski smiled. "Roger. Say, you gonna need some help over there?"

"No, I've got Tuong helping. I need you down there watching that approach."

"Good luck. See you later." He turned and jogged away.

I watched him disappear over the southern crest of the hill. Arnold Binkowski was from Massachusetts. He'd volunteered for RT Texas nine weeks ago after I lost my partner in a clusterfuck fire fight. Ski had only been to the bush with us twice, but both missions had been hot and he'd performed well under fire.

I silently complimented Ski's presence of mind about keeping our nose to the mission—our mission was to locate and recover Abe Duell. But from what I'd heard about the legendary Duell, he'd toss his chips in the center of the table anytime to save a Hmong life.

I'd learned from the pre-mission dossier that Abe Duell joined the International Volunteer Service, an American-sponsored agency, at age forty-eight. He'd come to the Plain of Jars here in Laos to teach new farming methods to the Hmongs—all for the grandiose salary of sixty-five dollars a month.

He was a skinny, five-foot-five-inch god to the Hmong. Since his arrival he'd not only worked tirelessly to help the people grow more productive crops, he'd also organized and set up the first schools for the Hmong. And, he'd implemented several medical aid stations throughout thirty some-odd tribes living in and around the Plain of Jars.

Duell had won the hearts of the Hmong people over the years because of his dauntless allegiance to them. He was a peaceful man—never carried a weapon. He didn't try to bother the Hmong with any sideline religious motives. What little help he got from government agencies he usually obtained through resourceful methods akin to begging, borrowing, or bartering.

Although IVS was U.S.-sponsored, it was way down the ladder of the higher priorities—CIA and Special Forces activities. During the past six years the achievements of Duell bordered on miraculous considering he'd done what he'd done virtually without support and without butting heads with the NVA, the Pathet-Lao, the CIA, or Special Forces.

My team had launched three days before from a secret SF forward operations base in Nakonphanom, Thailand. These missions were code-named Heavy Hook. I'd learned from the FOB commander, Major Helton, that Duell had been given a sacred name by the Hmong—Tan-Pop—which means "he who is sent from above." Now, the closest friend the Hmong people had ever known had suddenly disappeared without a trace.

When I returned to Chung, the grimace on his face told me the morphine was wearing off. I administered another Syrette, then looked around for the elders. They were gone.

"Tuong, where go papasans?"

He shrugged. "Don know."

"Come on," I blurted, while heading for the Shaman's hut. I knelt and looked inside. Nothing.

A few minutes later we found them gathered around a tree inspecting the branches. It was a disjointed guess that they were trying to find evidence of a new limb growing—something to substantiate my earlier proclamation.

I quickly confronted them, interrupting their horticulture tour. "Look, gents, I don't have all damn day! Chung is—"

"Ho!" The Shaman uttered, jabbing his open palm up to me like a city traffic cop. His eyes turned to Tuong as he poured out a long spiel while waving the small branch I'd given him.

Finally, the Shaman stopped. He squatted near the base of the tree and began scooping dirt away with his hands. He then placed the branch into the shallow hole, covered it, then stood, bowed, and walked away slapping his hands together. The other elders grinned at me, then trailed off behind the priest.

I frowned at Tuong. "What'd he say?"

Tuong grinned. "Him say is okay for you to ampoo . . . ampoo arm. Da say will bury arm here and when someday when Chung him die him musting be bury here same same place wid arm.

"Dat way him be join togeder when him go to up dar." He pointed upward. "All number-one, Sar Brett."

"Good! Come on. I'll need your help during this," I said, checking my watch; 1310 hours. I'd lost over an hour waiting for the jury to come in.

When we returned to Chung, his mother was seated, cradling his head in her lap, he was still conscious. Using Tuong, I explained to them what had to be done. I told Chung that he would have to be brave. I said that within a few days the pain he was enduring would be gone and that he would forever be a special symbol of courage among the Hmong.

Tears came to his eyes when he understood that I was about to remove his arm. His mother wiped the tears from his cheeks and tilted his head in her lap to look away from me.

I prepped the area above and below the elbow joint with more morphine, then folded my poncho over a small log and positioned it under his blackened arm to provide a solid surface for cutting. Before beginning I had Tuong tell the village spectators that this was a private ceremony and that the gods didn't want anyone watching. They quickly dispersed.

Then I instructed him to keep the flies fanned away from the arm while I worked and to hand me cups of hot water as well as a hot knife when I asked for it.

I took my bush hat off, then folded and tied a cravat around my forehead, Indian style, to keep sweat out of my eyes. I removed what few medical supplies I had in my rucksack and set them between me and the fire. My meager assortment of med supplies amounted to a bottle of iodine, a pint of serum albumin, two field pressure bandages, three extra cravats, five Syrettes of morphine, and a couple of amyl nitrate capsules. The one thing I needed most I didn't have—Ampicillin tablets.

Pulling the damp cloth away from the arm, I examined the wound. I decided to sever the arm a few inches above the elbow joint to make sure I cleared out all the infection. I'd try and make my cut in such a way as to leave a flap of skin to draw over the stump and secure.

Silently, I reviewed my intended procedure. I planned to make a circular cut completely around the arm, then use the top serated part of my knife to saw through the upper arm bone. My next task would be to stop the bleeding—I planned to cauterize the artery and veins using the other hot knife, then draw the flap portion of skin tightly over the stump and cauterize that. I wasn't sure how effective the cauterizing method would be, but without a suture kit, it was the only method I had.

Shock. I'd forgotten about the potential of shock and I damn sure didn't want to have to deal with that if I could help it.

"Tuong," I said, motioning at Chung's mother. "Tell her not to let Chung go to sleep and tell her that if he passes out to let me know right away. Roger?"

"What mean, passes ou?"

I searched my mind trying to find an explanation. "It means, it means . . . quick sleep."

As he turned to the mother I grabbed an amyl nitrate capsule and passed it to him. "Give this to her and tell her to break it open and hold it to Chung's nose if he goes into quick sleep."

While Tuong went through the explanation I opened several fresh cravats and field dressings and placed them on top of my rucksack for ready use.

"It okay, Sar Brett. Her understan," Tuong announced,

while tossing a pebble to shoo away the dogs and chickens.

I took a deep breath. "Okay, let's get this started." I began washing my hands while continuing. "Take that canteen cup and pour hot water from here down. Do it slow," I said, pointing along the black area of arm. I dried, then wrapped a cravat around my palm and carefully pulled a hot knife from the fire. Droplets of sweat tickled the back of my neck.

Tuong fanned the flies off the arm, then slowly poured a cup of hot water along the area near the elbow. I watched Chung for signs of pain reaction as the water flowed over the black arm. None.

Gripping the warm, crusted elbow with one hand, I sliced my hot steel into the dark skin, immediately sensing the putrid stink of searing, decayed flesh. I cut deeper until the blade intersected the bone, then rotated the knife around the small arm, cutting a flap section outward as I moved to the back side of the limb. I guided the blade back and forth, gnawing away the muscle. The warm greasy flow of blood melted through my fingers.

I turned the serated edge of the knife inward beneath the flap and dug deeper to find the bone again. I probed the edge upward to recess the area where I was going to cut the bone. Blood and decayed skin covered my blade. The salty sting of sweat blurred my vision.

"More water!" I muttered, blinking madly to clear my eyes.

Tuong hurriedly dipped the cup into the hot water pot. I released my bloody grip while he poured the hot liquid over the area of my incisions.

Again, I gripped the rotted flesh to steady the arm and began a rasping sawing motion. After several intense repetitions I felt the slender bone sever. I quickly cut through the remaining strings of skin and pulled the grotesque residue away, dropping it at my knees.

I jabbed the bloody knife back in the fire and gripped

the other waiting knife. I hurriedly pressed the wide side of the hot blade onto the bleeding stump and held it tightly over the vessels and veins. Scorched, melting flesh raped my nostrils.

Continuing to hold the blade in position with one hand I fumbled, trying to draw the slippery flap of skin around the stump. Finally, I pinched, pulled, and tugged it over the end and held it tightly while easing my blade from beneath the flap. I pressed the skin tighter against the stump while moving the blade around the raw edges of flesh to cauterize it.

"Ahee, oh, oh!" Chung groaned, as my hot blade seared more skin.

"Hold him steady! Almost *fini*!" I yelled, tossing the knife aside and reaching for the other. I gritted my teeth, trying to steady the writhing boy struggling away from the agony of my burning steel. I mashed the red blade harder over the skin fusing more flesh. Finally, after what seemed a smoldering eternity, I pulled away.

"Water, Tuong!"

Moments later we'd washed the stump, dried it, and checked it for signs of bleeding. I doused the dry area with iodine before wrapping it tightly with bandages, then I added an extra cravat wrap over the gauze.

I dragged my blood-cloaked arm over my wet forehead and slumped, listening to the wailing cries of the young Hmong boy clutched lovingly in his mother's embrace.

Brushing a tear from my eye I whispered, "If I believed in God and prayer, young warrior, I'd beg Him to give all your pain to me."

# Chapter 3

The village Shaman carefully wrapped the bloody, black scraps of the severed arm with leaves, then beckoned me to join him in the burial ritual. I declined, indicating that I needed to tend to Chung.

Tuong and I gently moved the boy into his hooch, then rigged a piece of parachute cord from the ceiling to suspend the stump of his arm upward. It was uncomfortable for the little guy, but it was important to keep the arm partially elevated for a while.

Using an empty Syrette, I had Tuong interpret while I showed Chung's mother how to administer morphine. I told her not to use it unless Chung was in "*beaucoup* pain." After checking his dressing for signs of bleeding I felt his forehead—warm and sweaty.

My primary concern now was the prevention of infection. I knew that without Penicillin he only had about a fifty-fifty chance of surviving, at best. He'd lived through the terror of a booby-trap explosion, the agony of gangrene, and the pain and horror of having his arm cut off— he deserved better odds.

I took a small packet of chewing gum from my shirt pocket and opened it. Smiling, I leaned and placed the white, gum square into his mouth. "You number-one," I said, flipping my thumb upward at him.

He grinned as he bit into the gum. Digging back into my pocket I pulled out another two packets of gum and gave them to his mother, nodding that they were for Chung.

I looked at Tuong. "Time for us to press on, babysan."

As I stood, Chung's mother said something to Tuong. "Wait, Sar Brett. Her wanting give you someting."

We watched for a moment as she scooped dirt away from an area near the corner of the hooch. She removed a wooden box, opened it, and took out a dark, folded piece of cloth. With graceful motions of her hands she unfolded the wrapping, revealing a bright, silver necklace. The circular pendant suspended from the chain was intricately etched with symbols and figures.

Holding the braided chain in both hands, she knelt, bowed her head, and extended her arms outward toward me without speaking.

"Is for you, Sar Brett. Is her way saying thanking you for sabing Chung," Tuong announced proudly.

"Well, we haven't saved him yet, partner. He needs Penicillin," I replied, darting a glance at Tuong, then back to Chung. I had no intention of taking the silver jewelry that was likely the family savings—but I didn't want to completely reject her gesture of gratitude.

I bowed my head, talking quietly out of the side of my mouth, "Tell her I say thanks for the beautiful gift, then tell her to keep it until I return in a couple of days."

Tuong frowned. "We come back dis place? Why?"

"Because Chung needs Penicill . . . medicine, and we're going to find it somewhere or Ho Chi Minh's not a skinny, little Communist."

When we exited the hut I saw the elders returning from the burial ceremony. I strode quickly toward them with Tuong running behind me.

"Ho!" I cried out, using the Shaman's best attention-grabbing word. He stopped and jerked a surprised look back to me. "Tuong, ask this gent if he knows where Tan-Pop is."

The Shaman's eyes widened as if I'd used a magic name. He talked with the other old men for a moment, then answered Tuong's inquiry with what was obviously a "we don't know."

"Him say no see Tan-Pop for long time. Him tink maybe him be dat way maybe go Khang Kai."

The pre-mission CIA briefing we'd received had eliminated Khang Kai as a likely place for Duell to be. At this point in time, CIA CAS agents had a handle on that area of influence and nobody had reported any sighting of Duell, but with the Agency handles sometimes fell off.

Duell had missed seven out of the last seven weekly radio contacts and that put him on the most wanted list with the CIA. I'd learned from our CIA intel briefer that the Agency had long regarded Duell as something of a thorn in their foot, and I was well aware that they had a habit of eliminating "thorns" post haste.

I'd asked the agent why they were so interested in maintaining Duell's continued ability to walk upright and process of healthy respiration. The agent pulled his sunglasses off, squinted, and blurted, "Well, that little prick has been a pain in the ass for years. You know, always bugging us for a plane, a chopper to medevac some sick Hmong or wanting medical supplies, and . . . shit you name it!

"But lately, well, ever since he got granted semi-god status with the Hmong, he's been the best source of reliable intelligence on NVA activity we've got in that neck of the woods. We even tried to put him on the payroll, but he wouldn't take the carrot. Ask me, I think he's a raving dumbass working for peanuts trying to grow sweet potatoes and corn. All he asks for is basic school supplies and medical supplies."

By 1600 hours, RT Texas was moving in strict-stealth formation along a portion of jagged, mountainous ridgeline that ran eastward toward the village of Na Dao. My map had proven inaccurate and I was glad we had our own seasoned tour guide: Tuong.

Commonly, Rham took the point, however, since Tuong had worked in this area some eighteen months ago, I felt it best to put him out front. Rham didn't argue with my decision, but it was obvious he didn't like being relegated to the tail gunner slot. Walking point had a certain prestige to it and the Cowboys valued the point slot as much as the team chess championship title.

The loud chatter of monkeys mingled with the excited squawk of birds nestled in the canopy above us as we crept through their damp habitat. I'd instructed Tuong to head us due east and avoid any paths or trails.

The dense undergrowth combined with an altitude of forty-five hundred feet MSL made movement slow and arduous. Half an hour into the trip, stumble, and fall trek, I halted the team near a limestone cliff that fell sharply away from a clearing on the north side of the lofty ridge.

The crisp, mountain air rushed through the clearing at about twelve to fifteen knots like a cool breath of air-conditioning over my sweaty body. I held both hands up, fingers spread, signaling fore and aft for the team to take ten in place. I moved to a rocky edge of the cliff and took out my field glasses to scan the northern valley.

Through the distant veil of blue haze below me, I could see a path paralleling a winding stream. The forested terrain was splotched with small, cultivated patches of slash-and-burn fields which the Hmong tribesmen carved out of the steep mountainsides to grow their two main crops—corn and opium. After the corn was harvested in August, the fields were sowed in opium poppies.

The corn provided basic sustenance for the Hmong families and their livestock, the opium was sold. The Hmong, realizing the instability of local currency, would only accept gold or silver for their opium; payment was usually in silver. The area study I'd read during our pre-mission prep said that when they accumulated significant amounts of gold or silver they would either fashion it into jewelry or bury it in secret caches to prevent invading forces from taking it.

The sharp crack of a branch sparked my senses. I quickly tucked the binoculars into my half-open shirt and turned, leveling my rifle toward the shadows behind me. I stood and edged closer to a cluster of vines drooping from the trees.

I gave a silent hand signal to Phan, then glanced to my right; Binkowski was leaning against a large, moss-covered rock. I picked up a stone and tossed it at him. As he turned, I held a finger to my lips, then pointed at the trees. Ski passed a signal on to Rham, then slowly stood and moved toward the bush.

Kneeling at the base of a tree I was still, watching, listening for the presence of enemy. Strong winds stirred through the jungle as I scanned the dim tree line. The shrill cries of cockatoos screeched from the shadows.

After moments of waiting and watching, I stood and lowered my rifle to rest on the shoulder sling—if it was Chuck, the NVA, they'd have been on us like fire ants on a dead cat by now.

"Brett, it's me," Ski whispered, moving out of the dark foliage. "What's up?"

Rham crept from the shadows beyond Ski and waved an all-clear signal.

"I heard something. Sounded close," I said, moving toward Ski.

Ski frowned. "Probably monkeys. We passed a couple back there before we stopped."

"It wasn't monkeys. Whatever it was, was heavy enough to break a good-sized stick," I muttered, taking a last look into the jungle. "Well, it's gone now," I finished, while motioning at Lok to get ready to head out.

"By the way, you never told me why we're going to this village . . . what's it called?"

"Na Dao," I answered, taking the binoculars from inside my shirt and shifting them into my side pants pocket.

"Okay, well, why are we going to Na Dao?"

"There's a medical aid station there that Duell set up."

Ski tilted his head slightly. "How did you know that?"

"They mentioned it in the mission briefing. Were you asleep during that part?"

"Of course not . . . it's just, well, heck . . . I can't remember everything. So, anyhow, why are we goin' there? Are you thinking Duell might be there?"

I started walking onward. "I doubt it, but it's my bet they'll have some Ampicillin and that's—"

"Ampicillin? Wait . . . why do we need, oh, I get it. It's for the boy. But that means, that means, well . . . damn!"

I stopped and turned. "Damn what, Arnold?"

Ski's hands waved at his side. "Well, well, this is all wonderful and noble of you, Brett, but even if we luck out and get the Ampicillin, that means we have to come back to the same village to give it to him."

I smirked. "Brilliant deduction, Watson. I think you're beginning to get the picture." I turned and motioned for the team to move out. "Let's move."

I felt Binkowski's exasperated breath at my back as I strode away. Ordinarily, Ski was cool in a tense field situation, but for some reason he'd been on the near side of jittery ever since we boarded the infil chopper at NKP. I didn't know what was bugging him but I made a silent note to myself to find out and correct it before his ice started melting. It was very possible I'd eventually have to split the team during part of our continued hunt for Duell— I wasn't about to risk a fourth-quarter argument about which play to run when the clock started winding down.

The steep terrain we'd traversed earlier began a gradual descent as we neared the village of Na Dao. My map marked the altitude of Na Dao at thirty-one hundred feet, the village was at the southeastern base of a mountain. A wide two-hundred-foot rock cliff rose like a jagged step-ladder off the northern edge of the hamlet.

I halted the team in a dense forested area and instructed Binkowski to make our 1730 radio contact with Sunburst, the day-monitor aircraft which worked the Prairie Fire AO. The message I gave Ski to transmit divulged only our grid location and the words, "negative contact; continuing mission." I deliberately avoided any mention of our civic action diversion or my efforts to locate a medical aid station.

While Ski coded the message for transmission, I took Tuong and found a good observation point near a large timber break on the mountainside. As we moved around the break, Tuong stopped abruptly and pointed down at an animal track.

"Big cat," he announced, squatting to study the paw impression in the dirt. The radius of the print was the size of a catcher's mitt.

I'd never seen a tiger during my missions into Laos, but I'd often heard their ominous, deep growls rasp through the night. The sound had a way of inspiring a man to flip his selector switch to full automatic.

Moments later we found some good concealment in a thicket. I pulled out my field glasses and slowly scanned the Na Dao area. The tall cliff above the village shielded the eastern region from the setting sun, leaving the hamlet cloaked in shadows. Lazy, white spirals of smoke rose from small, amber fires dotting the interior of the Hmong camp.

I noticed a large clearing on the southern side of the village about the size of a dog-leg football field. Tuong told me it was a landing strip for the CIA's favorite short-take-off, rough terrain, aircraft—the Turbo Porter. The grassy strip didn't appear recently used.

The lack of light combined with the distance obscured a clear view of movement in the village. I passed the binoculars to Tuong. "Tell me what you see."

Earlier, Tuong revealed to me that he'd been through this village only once during his operation in and around the Plain of Jars. I couldn't expect him to remember much about it and it was very possible that the aid station had been established after Tuong left the area. My concern right now was focused on trying to determine if Na Dao was occupied by the bad guys.

"No see Pat-Lao, no see Chuckie, Sar Brett," Tuong mumbled, while keeping the glasses fixed on the village. Finally, he turned and smiled. "All look okay."

I took the binoculars and peered back at the little town, then looked upward toward the cliff above it. I inspected what appeared to be a deep ledge skirting just beneath the summit. If the rock was solid along the ledge it would be the best night observation spot we could hope for.

I decided to try and find a good RON site somewhere along the cliff ledge and observe the village until first light. When the morning fog rolled in, we'd move down into the hamlet. I pointed to the area of cliff indentation and made sure Tuong knew where I wanted him to take us. He studied the area, then nodded.

"We go team now, eat chow, then come dark we do a little rock climbing," I said, glancing at my watch: 1805 hours. I winked. "You keep a sharp eye out for Tony the Tiger on our way back, Tonto."

"Who Tony-Tiger, Sar Brett?"

# Chapter 4

Moving silently through the damp cloak of a dark, purple night, RT Texas ascended the sloped backside of the cliff area, then edged downward toward the rocky shelf. I'd instructed the team to exercise maximum noise discipline and to be particularly careful not to kick rocks and stone chips loose during the short, angling descent to the ledge.

Rham crawled along the rim ahead of us and found a small cave near the end of the cliff. After evicting a squadron of bats from their hangar, he inspected the interior and motioned us inside. The cave was about as spacious as a Vietnamese elevator, but it was good cover and concealment despite the cramped quarters. As we crowded into the hole, I signaled Rham to remain outside and take first watch.

Seconds later Binkowski's agitated whisper grated the darkness. "Damn it, I think I just sat in a pile of shit!"

"Sorry, Arnold. This was the only penthouse they had left on short notice," I said, shifting my rucksack off and placing it by Lok. "What kind of shit is it?"

"How the hell do I know? Shit's shit as far as I'm concerned!" he coughed. "Can't you smell it? Surely—"

The Cowboys jolted with laughter.

"Y'all keep it down," I said, leaning closer to Ski. "Is it big lumps of shit or little balls?"

"Godammit, Brett, I've done just about everything you've ever asked me to do, but I'm not gonna feel up a pile of shit, okay!"

I didn't want to intentionally stir Binkowski's ire, but my concern right now was that we might have invaded some local ape's favorite bathroom. If whatever it was dropped by for a midnight deposit, the potential confrontation and noise could blow our cover.

"Okay, Ski, can you tell if it's big or small?"

"It's . . . it's little . . . it's little, squashy shit!"

The fetid stench of shit and sweaty bodies twisted through the cramped darkness like a screw through a cork.

"Try and clean yourself up, partner. I'll be outside with Rham. Keep the noise down in here."

I crept out the small opening and into the windy, night air. Rham lay prone along the white glow of the rocky ledge peering down toward Na Dao. I eased in beside him. Without speaking, he turned and nodded to indicate he hadn't seen anything. Returning to his vigil, he studied the dim silhouette of the village like a cat watches a still canary.

At age twenty-one, Pug was the oldest of my Yards. Several missions back we'd been shot out of a DMZ target by a hive of NVA. Somewhere in that swarming maze of 7.62 lead, Rham caught a round directly across the end of his nose. A doctor at 95th medevac hospital in Da Nang reformed the bloody proboscis, giving Rham the distinction of being the only pugnose Montagnard in Southeast Asia.

The soft rumble of thunder murmured in the distance. Pulling out my field glasses, I peered toward the quiet village and focused. I had started to tell Pug that he could move into the cave but decided he'd be better off out here.

Within moments the exodus of the other Yards began just as I'd expected. One by one they crawled into prone positions near me, leaving Ski banished to the cave.

Suddenly my gaze was caught by a cloaked, catlike figure crouching and moving slowly along the near side of the village. An arm stretched from beneath the hunched cloak holding what appeared to be a large bone.

Adjusting the binoculars, I followed the creature's cautious movement as it wove stealthily from hut to hut. It stopped and made a jabbing motion at each small structure. I nudged Tuong lying near me and pointed downward at the area while handing him the binoculars.

Taking the glasses, he studied the night stalker for a moment, then handed them back to me and grinned. "Dat saw-man. Him do same same ever nigh to keep away an-e-ma." Tuong's grin widened. "You know, an-e-ma. Liking Tony-Tiger," he whispered.

I nodded, took the binoculars, and watched the Shaman continue his anti-tiger ritual throughout the village. I thought to myself, "Too bad he doesn't have an anti-communist ritual."

At 2230 hours all was still quiet. I took Phan and Lok to set up a listening post thirty meters from where we'd entered the cliff ledge. Before returning to the team, I instructed them to position a Claymore mine on the other side of the boulder we'd selected as LP cover. It had dawned on me that although we had the best area of observation with our cliff vantage point, it was also a dead-end street if we got hit in our lofty RON.

When I got back to the main element of the team I decided that now was as good a time as any to run a psychiatric pulse check on Ski to try and find out what was making him so jittery.

I crouched entering the cave and was immediately hit with the permeative odor—essence of unknown animal shit.

My cough broke the dark silence just before my whisper. "How you doing, partner?"

"Just fuckin' wonderful! I used most of my water washing that stuff outta my pants. I only got about half a canteen left.''

I understood Ski's concern. In a common field environment we were very conservative with water use, but this area had no water shortage.

Sitting on my rucksack, I leaned forward with elbows on my knees. "That's no sweat, buddy. There's plenty of streams up here. You can fill your canteens in the morning. Be sure and use your purification tabs.''

"Roger," he replied, as I heard the loose metallic sound of his belt buckle rattle. "I'm going to put these pants back on even if they are wet.

"Brett, do you believe in omens?" he asked while shifting into his trousers.

"What, like superstition? Black cats? All that?''

"Yeah . . . only more.''

"Never though much about it.''

"Well, my grandmother kinda raised me and she was real big on it; omens and superstition, I mean.

"Once when I was a kid playin' in the backyard she was looking out the kitchen window and noticed me walk under a ladder out by the garage. Know what she did?''

"No.''

"She came outside and made me walk back under the ladder in a counterclockwise direction fifty-six times. I remember, I almost got dizzy doing it.''

I waited, thinking he was going to enlighten me about the significance of what he just said.

After a long pause he spoke. "Don't you want to know why she had me—"

"Okay. Why?''

"Because seven is a lucky number and it was eight days until the next full moon. Get it? Seven times eight is fifty-six.'' Ski's emphatic tone sounded like he'd just revealed the theory of relativity.

I decided to try and switch frequencies back to my intended pulse check. "I understand, Ski. Everybody has some hang-ups with that kind of thing." I paused, then casually asked if anything had been bugging him lately.

"That's exactly what's buggin' me, Brett!" He proclaimed in a loud whisper.

"What? You mean we walked under a ladder somewhere on this mission?" I retorted, hoping the humor would take some of the edge off his mood.

"No! Remember, we launched from NKP two days ago; November thirteenth nineteen sixty-nine, right?"

"Roger," I answered dryly.

"Well . . . now do you see?"

"Look, Arnold," I said, pushing upright off my knees. "It was pitch black when I crawled in here, and it's getting darker by the minute. What are you trying to—"

"Hold it, Brett," he intruded, moving closer to me. "Let me explain. My R and R begins on the twenty-sixth of this month. We launched on the thirteenth and twenty-six is thirteen doubled.

"That means I'm up against two unlucky numbers. You know of course that thirteen is an unlucky number? It's—it's like I'm facing a double-whammy or something!" He finished solemnly, "This is serious."

I'd had some revelation of Ski's superstitious nature one evening several weeks back while we were in Da Nang getting our sperm count lowered. I noticed Binkowski avoiding cracks in the sidewalk, which wasn't exactly easy to do considering the old city had more cracks than sidewalk. But I had no idea Ski's paranoia was this deep.

I reasoned that part of it had to do with preoccupation with his forthcoming R and R. I'd seen some transitions in guys when they were anticipating a break from the war or getting short. They got nervous.

It was obvious that a team of psychiatrists couldn't put a dent in Ski's lifelong habit, but I needed to do something to help him re-zero his psych-sights before he started getting too loose in his loafers. So far we'd been fortunate and not made hostile contact, but if and when that occurred, Ski needed at least fifty-two cards in his deck or he'd be dead.

"Yeah, partner. I know what you mean about superstition," I said emphatically. "My uncle used to race dirt-track stock-cars. He said the other drivers all believed the superstition that if a man had a number on his race car that would read like another number upside down, you know like a six or ninety-nine, he was doomed to crash and flip upside down."

"I've heard that," Ski said seriously.

"Well, my uncle told them that superstition was bullshit and painted a big bright, red eighty-one on the side doors of his racer."

"What happened?" Ski asked eagerly.

"Sure enough he flipped during the first race."

"See! I'm tellin' you there's something to this shi . . . to superstition, Brett, and you just as much as admitted it!

"Was your uncle hurt?"

I chuckled. "No, but he promptly changed the number on his car to thirty-seven before he raced again."

Pausing, I changed my tone to objective. "Now, the way I understand it is, you're up against two thirteens and that's what's got you bothered. Right?"

"Bothered is a mild word for it, Brett. This could be well, well . . . fatal. You know?"

"Okay. Obviously, I can't change the launch date, but if you can live with one thirteen then I have a plan to cut your bad luck by fifty percent."

"Great!" he blurted through the darkness. "What is it?"

I explained to Ski that as of right now I was canceling his R and R.

"What? . . . Wait! Isn't, isn't that a little extreme?" he whined.

"Maybe. But not as extreme as a sucking chest wound." I told him that since the twenty-sixth was the real "double

whammy'' I figured he could face the heat with the bad
launch date.

Resting my case, Ski pondered my bubble-gum and glue
effort to de-hex the dilemma.

My personal opinion about luck and superstition was
that they were luxuries. They didn't have anyplace influ-
encing the conduct of a war, but if it helped my partner
get his head re-arranged I was prepared to play the pseudo
game.

Finally, he reluctantly agreed with my rationale. Only
time would tell if he'd allowed my pitch to sink in. I hoped,
in the meantime, that he didn't run into a black cat crossing his trail before things took hold and he got his mind
off the subject completely.

"Okay, but there's one thing still buggin' me and you
already know what it is, I think. Our mission is to find
Abraham Duell and instead we're getting involved helping
that kid and—''

"You leave that to me!'' I responded quickly. This was
the second time I'd heard this broken record recital and I
was tired of it. "Understand this, Binkowski. Abe Duell
is a grown man who knew right up front what he was getting into over here. He may be dead by now for all we
know.

"But that little boy is alive and I don't give a flying fuck
how many thirteens, witch doctors, or evil eyes get in my
way, I'm pressing on to give him every chance I can. . . .''
I caught my voice slipping from empathy to anger.

Taking a deep breath I added, "That means Ampicillin,
and I don't need any more reminders about Duell. You
copy?''

"Roger,'' he muttered.

The rank stink of feces invaded my nostrils again. I
lifted my rifle and moved toward the cave opening. "I'm
going to get back on watch. I put Phan and Lok out on
LP. I want you to go check on them.''

# Chapter 5

Jagged fingers of lightning tore through the midnight sky, silhouetting the notched mountains rimming Na Dao like a broken-edged bowl. Within seconds the sky unloaded a cold, pelting deluge. Rham, Tuong, and I lay cloaked in ponchos along the cliff awaiting Ski's return from the LP.

Ski had been gone for almost an hour on what should have taken no more than twenty minutes. Slowly a trough of water began streaming down and along the ledge soaking into my fatigue pants. The heavy rain obscured the dim village.

I nudged Rham, then Tuong, and pointed toward the cave indicating it was time to move inside. After positioning Tuong at the mouth of the cave as vigil, I moved cautiously out into the windy pall of rain to look for Binkowski.

Nearing the LP I saw the poncho-clad profiles of Lok and Phan hunkered beneath swaying limbs at the corner of the boulder. Their rifle muzzles jutted up from their ponchos like empty flagstaffs.

"Lok box!" I whispered loudly as I moved closer.

Turning, Lok slipped the hood of his shroud back. "Lok box open." He whispered answering my challenge.

"Where Ski?" I asked, moving closer.

He blinked. "No see Ski, Sar Brett."

Thirty minutes later we'd searched the tangled night in a thirty-meter half-moon zone around the LP. No sign of Ski. The steep terrain and unrelenting downpour made footing in the area extremely slippery. Although I didn't want to admit it I knew it was possible Binkowski had taken a wrong turn and slid halfway down the mountain in the darkness. And it was understandable, considering our tactical situation, that he'd avoid yelling out for help if he was injured.

We returned to the LP and huddled beneath a group poncho, waiting.

At 0215 hours I decided to continue a solo search for Ski. I told Phan and Lok to maintain their position, and if Binkowski showed up to have him stay in place until I got back. I couldn't risk the possibility of Ski being unconscious and vulnerable to the predators inhabiting the region. Laos was crawling with snakes, tigers, apes, and worse—Pathet-Lao and NVA.

I carefully retraced the trail leading from the cliff to the LP looking for any area that stemmed from the corridor that could have diverted Ski's direction. Thunder boomed and lightning lit the black rain gusting through the jungle like a short-circuited strobe light.

Using my rifle as a probe, I crept off the small path and into thick vegetation near the base of a rocky shaft. This appeared to be the only place Binkowski could have diverted from the trail. Wait-a-minute vines raked over me, snagging and tearing at my poncho as I dug my way into the murky thicket. I deliberately broke branches, clawing a wide path of vines aside to help guide me back.

Suddenly my wet fingers grasped the thick girth of a large snake in the blackness. The scaly texture quickly spiraled, tightening a grip over my hand. Jerking madly away I stumbled backward, thrashing my rifle barrel blindly into the limbs ahead of me. I continued my reckless retreat, then slipped, dropping square on my ass in the mud.

"Shit! You're going to fuck around out here and be a casualty yourself, Yancy!" I muttered in the darkness while pushing myself upright with my rifle.

It appeared that trying to find Ski was quickly becoming a "needle in a muddy haystack" routine. I turned and groped through the dark, tangled undergrowth toward the trail.

Winding my way slowly back to the LP I decided to wait until first light, then deploy the team in an overlapping search pattern. It seemed Murphy's Law was trying to take another bite out of RT Texas.

Ten meters from the boulder I stopped dead in my tracks and squinted through the rain in awe. There, just a stone's toss in front of me was the unmistakable, Neanderthal profile of Arnold Binkowski standing beside Phan and Lok. With his poncho on he looked like a monk version of the Jolly Green Giant.

I plodded ahead, half mad, half elated to see him. "Where the hell have you been, Arnold?"

"Brett! Am I glad to see you. I, I think I've found a friend and—"

I flared. "This isn't international pen-pal week, Binkowski! I've been clawing my way through monsoon mud, vines, and snakes trying to find you. Now where—"

"Okay, okay . . . calm down," he blurted, taking a step backward. "Let me explain, I'll tell you. I—I was coming down here just like you told me and suddenly I looked up and saw this Hmong fella swing down right out of a tree, holding a crossbow and wearing nothing but leather underwear and a serape.

"Scared me shitless for a minute; I almost blew him away, and anyhow he did this bow and started grinning. He laid his crossbow down . . . I—I guess to show me he wasn't meaning me no harm and—"

"Hold it! Have you been smoking opium, Binkowski?"

"Absolutely not, Brett. I promise. Never in my life. This is for real, partner."

For the next ten minutes, as we walked back toward the cave, I listened with strained patience as Binkowski unfolded the story of his guided journey into the catacombs of the mountain we'd chosen as our observation spot.

He said that although he couldn't understand a word the man was saying, the man was friendly and obviously enthused about leading him to something. They slipped down into the tunnels of the mountain using an old lantern to light the way. Ski estimated they traveled about one hundred meters into the core of the mountain winding through tunnels and occasionally descending a shaft by ladder. In several places during the descent, the Hmong took Ski's hand to lead him around what Ski felt were booby-traps.

When they arrived at a big, rough, domed room the skinny tribesman grinned and pointed out a large weapons cache, with old flintlock rifles, AK-47s, chi-com rocket launchers, M-16s, and an abundance of assorted ammo. Then the Hmong removed a small section of rock from a wall, pulled out a wooden box the size of a U.S. ammo container, and opened it, revealing a huge quantity of silver coins. The man then picked up the box, bowed his head and handed it to Ski. Ski said he promptly gave it back to the man.

I stopped. "Okay, if all this is on the level, Arnold," I said, wiping the rain off my face, "Then why didn't you take it?"

"Why? . . . Well, I, I don't know why. But, but I couldn't just take a bunch of money for nothin'. Heck, I don't even know why he wanted to show me all that!" He answered, pointing quickly toward the mountain. "Shit! Maybe he's the one's been smokin' opium!

"I was totally stumped, Brett. Dumfounded. You have to remember that I didn't have any commo with this guy. I know it's bizarre, but surely you don't think I'm making this up?"

I studied Binkowski's dark face wishing I could see his pupils. He was right about one thing: his "Journey to the

center of the Earth'' story was bizarre. It seemed too out-
landish to be fabricated.

I pulled the drawstrings of my poncho hood tighter, then
adjusted my rifle sling to position my muzzle downward.
''Okay, okay. But how'd you get back here?''

''He brought me back.''

''Fine. Where is he now?'' I questioned.

Arnold cast a futile look off into the rainy night. ''I—I
don't know. When we moved out of that thick stuff over
there I looked around and he was gone.''

Walking onward I remembered that our intel briefing
had divulged that a Hmong general named Vang Pao was
operating in and around the Plain of Jars. It was believed
that he'd amassed large caches of supplies and weapons in
various locations throughout the mountains as a kind of
reserve security blanket just in case U.S. aid suddenly
ended. Reportedly, the stockpiles included both U.S. supplies and any weapons and ammo he captured during his
frequent assaults on NVA and Pathet-Lao positions.

General Pao's insight proved to be center target—I re-
called that the last issue of Stars and Stripes had mentioned that Congress had adopted the Cooper amendment
which was to put an immediate end to all U.S. military
aid to Laos.

As we approached the pale, crusty edge of the cliff a
thought hit me like a split-second thunderbolt. I halted,
turning face to face with Ski. ''Did you see any medical
supplies in the cache?''

''You don't fucking belive me, do you!'' he said, blinking.

''Yes, I fucking believe you! Did you see any medical
supplies?''

''I—I don't know. I don't think so. It wasn't like he was
taking me there to show off his arsenal. I didn't get a tour
of the whole place. Basically, he was just wanting to give
me the box of silver.

"And to tell you the truth, I wish now I'd taken it! At least I'd have something to back up my story."

I reached forward and grabbed his shoulder. "Look, partner, I believe you. I'm thinking there could be some Ampicillin in there in a medical kit or something. It's just a long shot," I said releasing my grip.

"Maybe . . . you know, Brett, there's something that's buggin' me about this little Hmong guy."

"What?"

"Well, I was wondering on the way back here why he was carrying a crossbow when he had all that assortment of guns available to him. Seems stupid. I mean, there musta been a hundred rifles or more in there."

I agreed; the same thought had crossed my mind, but right now the possibility of medical supplies was the more critical question churning through my head. Perhaps it was an optimistic guess on my part, but it was reasonable to assume that any cache which included American supplies would probably have M-5 med kits. Those kits came standard with the one thing I needed most right now—Ampicillin tablets.

I squinted, feeling a hard gust of rain-laced wind sting my face. "Where is the tunnel entrance? Can you find it again?"

"No way, Brett. It was way on the other end of this mountain and pitch black all the way there and—"

"Think, partner. If you can get us into the general zone we'll find it. That means we could skip the village recon tomorrow."

"Roger, I'll try and remember everything I can but—"

"That's good enough, buddy. Now let's get out of this fucking rain."

Upon return to the cave I hit Tuong with two questions: why would a Hmong be traveling at night with a crossbow when he had rifles available and why would he be trying to give Binkowski silver?

Tuong was as stumped as Ski and I about the silver, but

his reasoning about the crossbow made sense. He said the warrior was more than likely a roving sentinel for Vang Pao. Carrying a crossbow was a ruse just in case he accidentally encountered a Pathet-Lao patrol—the patrol would think he was a non-militant Hmong simply hunting for food thereby avoiding any hassles with the Communists. Later he passed on any intelligence he learned about size, strength, and direction of movement of the patrol to General Pao via the local grapevine.

The disguise Tuong described was somewhat akin to the way Buddhist monks in Vietnam would stroll through an area unchecked, then scrutinize our troop movement and report it to the local VC rice burners.

I pulled my cravat over my nose bandit-style to block out the lingering stink and stretched out near Rham to sleep. As my eyes closed, Binkowski broke squelch. "Brett," he said in a loud whisper, "I just thought of something else about that big cache. There were cases of C-rations stacked along one wall.

"I remember because I started to ask him if I could get a can of beans and franks out of one of the boxes. You know how I love beans and franks."

"Yes, I know. So, why didn't you ask for some?"

"Be . . . because I'd just refused a whole box of silver and—and I thought he might think I was stupid . . . weird, if I let him know I liked beans and franks more than money. I mean, wouldn't you think that was stupid if someone did that to you?"

"Maybe. But right now all I want you to think about is trying to remember the way back to the tunnel entrance. Roger?"

His voice wilted. "Roger. I'm thinking."

I laughed. "In a way I'm glad you didn't bring any beans and franks back with you."

"Why?"

"Think about it, Arnold. We've got enough stink in this

bungalow already without your famous napalm bean farts.''

He coughed. "Yeah, guess you're right. They even bother me sometimes. You know, I'd give anything for a cheeseburger right now.''

I baited Ski while pulling a nylon poncho liner from my pack. "We're moving out at first light. If you find that cache for me, I'll buy you a rucksack full of cheeseburgers when we get back to NKP.''

As I pulled the liner over me I heard what sounded like the muffled repetitive thunder of Arc-Light explosions in the distance.

Lying in the damp darkness I thought about Chung. His childhood had been brief. He'd been surrounded by wars since his birth. Now he was flat on his back in a thatched hut fighting for his right to live. I hadn't done any praying since losing my son and I wasn't about to start now. Closing my eyes I made a silent pledge: "I won't let you down, young warrior. I won't let you down.''

# Chapter 6

A gentle nudge woke me at the same time a damp hand cupped over my mouth; it was our team method of waking each other when something was too close to risk a whisper or the chance of an abrupt reaction.

Rising, I leaned and performed the same cautious waking procedure on Rham. I gripped my rifle and crawled toward the dim peak of morning light at the cave entrance. The rain had subsided to a light drizzle.

Tuong lay prone with his CAR-15 readied. He pointed outward and toward the left side of the cave mouth. My senses strained trying to hear or see anything. Droplets of water fell softly off the rocks extending above the cave entrance.

Edging closer to Tuong, I pulled a branch slowly aside trying to get an unobscured view. I'd counted on the LP to give us some advance warning if Pat showed up, but the absence of Phan or Lok indicated that whatever was out there had either slipped by them or killed them on the way in.

Suddenly an arrow was tossed near the cave mouth. I tensed, looking closer. The arrow was broken in the center and lay just four feet in front of me. I glanced at Tuong to read his reaction.

Tuong gave me a quick thumbs up response, crawled

forward, and slowly pushed the muzzle of his CAR-15 out
under the brush. I guessed it was his gesture to indicate
he wasn't going to fire.

Within seconds, the barechested reincarnation of Co-
chise duck-walked into view with his crossbow. He
grinned, placed his crossbow over Tuong's rifle barrel,
then pressed his hands together, praying style, and nodded.

"That's him, that's him!" Ski whispered loudly. "Hi.
Come on in," he said, leaning forward and pressing his
knee onto my butt while he motioned the tribesman inside.

The Hmong darted a glance around the cliff, then
crawled into the cave and squatted. Water streamed down
his face and torso as he nodded while grinning at us and
waving at Ski.

"Brett, this is the guy who took me to the cache."

"Great. Now how 'bout getting your knee outta my ass.
Tuong, find out what's up with our visitor."

As Tuong chattered quietly with the Hmong, I turned
and told Rham to go out and check on Lok and Phan. As
he moved forward, crouching, Tuong told Rham that the
tribesman said, "Pat-Lao here." Rham nodded and exited.

By 0550 hours we'd moved out of the cave, linked up
with the other team members, and were headed eastward
along the thickly vegetated limestone base at the upper
mountain ridge following our new volunteer guide, Fayden.

Tuong's guess that Fayden was a roving spy for Vang Pao
turned out to be right. The surprise came when we learned
that he was Chung's father—he'd had to flee his village to
avoid conscription, or death, at the hands of the local
"Pathet-Lao" recruiters.

Fayden subsequently joined General Pao's army and was
assigned solo sentinel duty in the area he knew best; a
ten-mile radius around his village. Occasionally, at night,

he was able to visit his family and bring food to them. Just after we departed the hamlet he'd learned from a villager that a big American had saved his son's life.

The silver that Fayden tried to give Ski was his small, personal fortune as gratitude for saving his son—he'd mistaken Binkowski for me. When Tuong informed him that it was me who'd performed the amputation he lit up, smiling and nodding as if he now understood why Ski would not accept the silver.

Fayden was also the cache-custodian for Pao's local arms stockpile. He gladly agreed to take us there when Tuong told him we hoped to find medicine to help Chung. Our guide didn't know if the stockpile contained medical supplies, but he said there were many boxes and crates in the cave. When I drew a cross in the dirt and told Tuong to ask if any of the boxes had that symbol on them painted in red, Fayden nodded affirmatively. My spirits jumped. We hadn't rung the bell yet, but the hammer was coming down.

The less exhilarating news was that ''Pat-Lao'' had entered the area two days ago and Fayden believed they were conducting a search for the weapons stockpile.

We learned that General Pao had relocated his main element on the western end of the Plain of Jars after a massive combined Pathet-Lao and Vietminh assault on his headquarters in Na Khang back in late February. Territorial supremacy in northern Laos was always like a kinetic see-saw brick fight, and right now we were sitting in the zone that represented the low end—the Communists, at least for the moment, were running free in our area of interest.

During the conversation I'd deliberately avoided asking Fayden anything about Abraham Duell, choosing to wait until later. I didn't want our guide to think that I had any priorities right now other than helping his son. It was possible, and understandable, that a father desperate for his child's survival, would lie to prevent anything that might loosen his fragile grip on hope.

At 0620 hours the drizzle began to subside, leaving the jungle veiled with a thin haze. Fayden led us out of the heavy brush and onto a narrow, tree-shrouded path that skirted the eastern portion of the mountain. Cool winds, laced with a strange, faint smell of smoke, whipped through the dim jungle.

I'd altered our normal route of march and positioned Tuong ahead of me, behind Fayden, just in case it became necessary to communicate with our guide.

Movement on the path was much easier than the arduous vine-strewn zone we'd just chewed through. But jungle corridors were danger areas—I usually avoided them like cactus. My former One-One, Will Washington, said trails gave him "path-o-phobia" and I was starting to feel that prevailing, neurotic itch.

A few meters down the path, Tuong turned and gave me that silent "are-you-sure-about-this" look. I nodded, reasoning that Fayden knew what he was doing and if there were any booby-traps, he had the keys. The other side of the coin was ambushes; the side I was trying not to think about.

Tuong dropped swiftly to one knee, jabbing an arm out to his side and down. I dropped, tensing my trigger finger and immediately passed the signal on to Lok.

A second later Tuong whirled, shot me the finger, and pointed into the high ground-bush off the right side of the path. His finger sign was a team signal indicating we were about to "get fucked" if we didn't get off the trail fast.

I quickly turned, finger-signaled Lok, and pointed into the bush. I'd lost sight of Fayden but figured it was him who alerted Tuong. I dug my way carefully into the thicket trying not to break any tell-tale branches in my wake.

Kneeling well-concealed behind a large elephant-ear plant, I took a grenade from my harness, loosened the pin

slightly for a quick pull, and placed it on the ground at
my knees.

I hawk-eyed the trail, searching for signs of movement
through the dim haze. There was no time to position a
Claymore. My team SOP on hasty ambushes and targets
of opportunity required the team to hold fire unless I initiated contact or the enemy fired on us. This time, if it
was an enemy coming down the street, I'd let them pass
rather than risk compromising our position. But if they
spotted us it was *sin-loi*—we'd cut them apart like a machete through rotten bananas.

The smell of his cigarette alerted me a second before
my eyes saw the dark, square-capped profile of the point
man. His hat looked like an old, French-style Havelock
cap. He strolled into view, stopped, looked back up the
trail, and jabbered something; no pack, AK at shoulder
arms. The absence of back packs indicated this was a small
satellite patrol working off a larger element.

There was no mistaking what he was smoking—I'd
smelled it many times—Ruby Queen always stunk like a
burning rattail.

"Kinda laid back this morning aren't you, Punky?" I
whispered under my breath, keeping my rifle muzzle
aimed at his slouched torso.

Soon, several other motley-garbed Pats ambled down
the trail with all the enthusiasm of a Mississippi road gang.
Four men total.

I squinted at the trail surface trying to see if our boot
cleats had left any tracks. The matted, leafy surface told
me that tracks were unlikely but I couldn't be sure.

The men talked for a moment, then continued on. They
were obviously feeling no inhibition about danger. They
were so close I could nail them all with one burst.

They were dressed in assorted military garb that looked
like the grab bag costume party variety but all carried late-
model Kalashnikov AKs and wore the new eight-pouch

magazine vest. Only the first man wore a Havelock. The others had folded black or OD scarfs circling their heads.

I waited for several minutes after the last man was out of sight, hoping that the tail element of my team stayed concealed and quiet until they were gone.

Taking a deep breath, I recovered my grenade, stood, and eased quietly to the edge of the path. Within seconds Fayden came scurrying down the trail and waved us onward.

Less than fifty meters later he led us off the trail into a steep, rocky area that contoured around the base of a cliff. Looking down a thousand feet below I could see the distant valley blanketed with thick fog. The sky was a dark, swollen mass of thunderheads moving slowly like a restless herd of Black Angus.

I checked my watch—0650 hours—then moved forward and asked Tuong to find out how much farther we had to go. As it turned out we were less than twenty meters from the cache entrance.

When we reached the cave mouth I told Tuong to move inside with Fayden and wait while I dispersed the remainder of the team as security along a portion of the route we'd just traversed.

I instructed Ski to contact Sunburst, day monitor aircraft, and give them a short, "negative contact, continuing mission" situation report. In previous contacts, base hadn't transmitted any traffic to us. Inwardly I was hoping we'd eventually get a message saying that Duell had been located. CCN had inserted two other teams, RT Kansas and RT Missouri, into the southern and central AO.

In addition, the CIA, CAS agents and Vang Pao's forces were all tuned-in to the search. It may have been my displaced sense of optimism but it seemed that somebody should find Abe Duell soon.

"I'm leaving my ruck here," I said to Ski, placing it behind the boulder he'd selected as cover. "You'd better

put out a Claymore just in case the Bowery boys hook
back this way.

"If they do, waste 'em! There's no exit up here, copy?"

"Roger. I—I guess this means I'm not—not going in
with you . . . in the cave I mean?"

"That's right. Not unless you're a split personality, Arnold," I answered, shifting my rifle sling over my neck
and peering along the narrow rocky trough we'd just come
up.

I stood and tapped his shoulder. "Keep a sharp eye,
partner. Probably going to rain pretty quick," I said,
crouching to move away.

"Brett, would you do me a favor?"

"What?"

"I'd sure like to have a can of those beans and franks
if it's not too much trouble."

I winked. "Roger, buddy."

Lightning ripped through the dark sky as I returned to
the cave and we began our descent. The method they'd
used to conceal the tunnel entrance was clever. The entrance had been dug in the top of a ledge. The back of the
cave was covered with a flat, circular rock.

After sliding the rock aside like a man-hole cover we
climbed up onto the ledge, then dropped about five feet to
the tunnel. Fayden lit a lantern using a packet of OD
matches and led us deeper into the tight, winding passage.

A hundred feet down the damp, musty corridor he
stopped and squatted, holding the light near the floor.
Peering over Tuong's shoulder I saw the Hmong pointing
to a trip wire which was elevated about four inches off the
dirt. Using my flashlight I noticed a horizontal tin can,
about C-ration size, which had been pressed into the clay
wall of the tunnel. Inside the can was an M-26 grenade
with the pin missing. The inner surface of the can kept the
detonation spoon in position until some hapless intruder
snagged the wire and jerked the grenade free.

We stepped carefully over the wire and continued onward about a minute to another booby-trap. This one was even more awesome. If an intruder somehow managed to evade the first trap, he didn't stand a snowball's chance in a cheerleader's crotch with the second one.

Fayden turned sideways, edging slowly around a large rock in the center of the path. He turned, holding one hand up to us emphasizing stop. He then raised his lantern toward the tunnel roof and grinned. There, recessed into the arched ceiling just inches above my head were a dozen pointed, bamboo stakes aimed to skewer anyone who stepped on the rock.

Tuong turned and smiled. "Is number-one, Sar Brett?" he asked gleefully.

I frowned. "Wonderful, fucking wonderful," I replied while looking down to make sure my boots were well away from the rock.

After passing the latest Hmong multiple-skewering appliance I was silently appreciative that Binkowski hadn't remembered how to get us into this obstacle course.

Within moments we reached what appeared to be the end of the tunnel. Fayden stretched upward and removed several boards from the ceiling, then reached inside and pulled down a knotted rope ladder.

I held Tuong's rifle while he followed Fayden up and into the hole. After handing our weapons up to Tuong I climbed inside and waited while Fayden began lighting several other lanterns.

The room was about the size and rough shape of a Quonset hut and a half. Ski's estimation of the arsenal was only partially correct.

"Wow, dis sum-ting else!" Tuong said, looking around.

"Roger, babysan," I replied, walking to a long, makeshift rifle rack while Fayden continued his lighting process.

I lifted an AK and ran my fingers along the receiver feeling a light coat of oil. I replaced the AK and glanced around at the assortment of rifles. In addition to an ample supply of AKs and M-16s there were M-2 carbines, forty-five caliber grease guns, a Japanese Arisaka carbine, and a couple of old French MAT499 submachine guns.

All the rifles appeared immaculately clean. It was apparent that Fayden performed his part-time job as armorer well. If I assumed that Vang Pao had ammo to go with all the weapons then the assemblage could easily arm approximately 150 men.

We followed Fayden toward the distant end of the cave where he lit another lantern, illuminating a huge quantity of varied boxes and crates all neatly stacked in rows. I moved through the chest-high rows of LRPRs, C-rations, and mortar-round crates following Fayden's hurried steps down a long aisle. I noticed several boxes of Claymores, LAWS, 5.56 and 7.62 ammo but saw nothing that indicated medical supplies.

At the end of the aisle, Fayden reached and drew back a canvas curtain revealing a dozen boxes with a large, red cross stamped on the side.

"Ya-ying! Ya-ying!" he blurted loudly pointing at the boxes.

"Outstanding, Fayden. You did good, buddy," I said, leaning my rifle against a crate. I reached and pulled the flaps of a box open. A sharp odor hit me just before my fingers touched the thin, brittle texture of something.

"What the hell is this?" I muttered, brushing dried leaves away from the top of the contents. "Tuong, bring that lantern here."

Tuong brought the glow of the lantern closer, talking as he moved. "Sar Brett, I'm tink maybe you no under—"

"Wait! This isn't . . ." I stopped in mid-sentence while picking up a dark, yellow block about half the size of a brick. "What is this?" I asked, turning first to Fayden, then to Tuong holding the block out. "It's damn sure not—"

"Dat what I'm try tell you, Sar Brett. Fayden, him say dis ya-ying."

A frown gripped my face. "Okay. What the hell is ya-ying?"

"It same same like for smoke. Feel good. You know, smoke in pip."

I lowered myself slowly and sat on a crate while staring at the block in my hand. "Opium! We came here for fucking opium?"

# Chapter 7

I only half-listened as Tuong gave me an unsolicited class in the fine points of the Hmong opium industry. He informed me that the best opium in the world was cultivated by the Hmong. And, although the Hmong condemned recreational usage of the drug, they always retained ten percent of their annual harvest to use for medicinal purposes—mainly to ease the suffering of those about to die.

A helpless sense of defeat kept gouging at me. It pissed me off that I'd let something fall through the cracks in our translation process. Fayden had done his duty: he brought us to the place that had boxes with a red cross on them—just like I'd asked for. Because of my failure we'd come all this way and all we had to show for it was guns and ya-ying.

To make things worse, my original plan to enter the village and search the aid station now had holes in it. With the Pathet-Lao in town we'd be stepping straight into a nest of snakes if we tried to enter Na Dao.

Fayden's expression had gone from happy to grim. I figured it mirrored the look on my face.

I stood and tossed the brick back into the box. Fayden looked at the box, then at me with a hard questioning frown.

There was no sense in concealing the truth. ''Tuong,''

I said, turning away to study the other assorted boxes. "Tell him this is not what we need. We're back at square one."

As Tuong went through the explanation I walked among the rows inspecting and looking for any indication of med supplies. Nothing.

"Sar Brett, him say no understan what we nee. And . . . maybe I no understan."

I turned, glanced over to Fayden, then down at Tuong. "Okay, gang. I'll try to explain it better this time."

I took a small, plastic bottle of malaria tablets from my aid pouch, opened it, and removed one of the white pills. I explained that what we needed looked like the tablets which I displayed in my palm. After returning the pill to the bottle I removed a pen from my pocket and wrote the word A-M-P-I-C-I-L-L-I-N on the side of a box in big letters. Then I reached out and held Fayden's palm up and carefully spelled the word on his hand. I did the same with Tuong, then spoke the word slowly, taking care to accent each syllable.

"Understand . . . Am . . . pi . . . cill . . . in. Am . . . pi . . . cill . . . in," I repeated.

Tuong spoke the word easily, then coached Fayden through it several times.

"Tuong, tell him this is medicine we need for Chung. The white tablets called Ampicillin. Okay? Make sure he understands."

The Hmong nodded, then stared at his palm and spoke what was perhaps his first English word.

"Ampa . . . silly. Ampa . . . silly," he said, darting a smiling glance to each of us then back to his hand.

"Close enough, Fayden. That's good. Ask him where he thinks we can find Ampa-silly, Tuong," I said, using Fayden's version of the word.

Squatting, the Hmong frowned, drew one hand to his mouth and concentrated on the word I'd inked into his

palm. His head tilted upward, looking at the top of the
cave and then around the room.

He looked at the stack of opium boxes, then back to his
hand as if trying to decipher the difference.

I decided to try a two-birds-one-stone question. "Tell
him that Tan-Pop will know where to find Ampa-silly.
Then ask him if he knows where Tan-Pop is."

Fayden responded with smiles and rapid-fire chatter after Tuong's question. Saying "Tan-Pop" several times, he
then shrugged and concentrated on his palm again. He
turned it down to view the back of his hand as if he expected the word to transpose on the other side.

"Him say Tan-Pop number-one. But not know where
is."

Leaning against a stack of boxes I pushed my bush hat
back on my head feeling frustration grip me tighter.

With a sudden springing movement, Fayden jumped to
his feet and scurried across the room to a shadowy area.

We followed and watched him methodically remove a
pile of small rocks from a hole in the cave wall.

He took out a box, squatted at our feet and opened it to
show us his silver. I listened while he spoke loudly to us
and pointed emphatically upward. At first I thought this
might be a repetition of the effort he'd made to give Ski
his silver.

My words hurried asking Tuong for a translation.

"Him say can maybe talk sil-ber and go buy Am-pa-
cill from Cor-see-kon."

"Cor-see-kon?" I repeated. "Dammit this isn't Main
Street where you just run down to the corner drugstore!"

"I'm only tell what him say, Sar Brett."

"Well, why does he think this guy Cor-see-kon has
Ampicillin? Ask him!"

A couple of sentences later I'd discovered that Cor-see-
kon was the disjointed pronunciation for the word Corsicans. They were the middlemen opium buyers that came
into the Plain of Jars every year during the growing sea-

son. They usually arrived in early October and stayed until after the harvest in January. I remembered that our CIA area briefing specialist had remarked, "Corsicans are to France as the Sicilians are to Italy."

It was apparent that Fayden knew where they were located and that he believed they would have the medicine we needed.

Thus far I'd drawn a blank on my efforts and I didn't feel like signing a quick purchase order on what might amount to little more than another proverbial reckless duck pursuit. But, after further questioning, I learned why Fayden felt certain the Corsicans would have medicine.

In order to gain favor with the Hmong, the Frenchmen would always come into a large growing area and distribute trinkets, canned food, and medicine to the locals. They were like the fur traders of early frontier America, giving the Indians blankets, beads, and liquor, then shisting them. Some of the buyers were believed to be French Army deserters and other "stay-behinds" who took up the opium trade after the fall of Dien Bien Phu.

The Hmong had been uneasy allies with the French since the early 1900s when French troops often provided them protection from marauding Chinese bandits known as Black Flags. The protection was really more of a practical economic requirement than it was a gesture of altruism—Black Flags targeted Hmong opium and Hmong opium was a lucrative French export.

Realizing that Fayden knew what he was doing, and was in fact doing all he could to help his son, I decided his idea was somewhere between a "maybe" and feasible—at any rate it seemed like the only viable alternative. I agreed with his plan to make a solo journey to the Corsicans.

To prevent a possible compromise of our presence to anyone, based on the word I'd written on his palm, I had Fayden rub the ink off his hand. Then I verbally rehearsed him until he could correctly pronounce both Penicillin and

Ampicillin. I estimated that the word Penicillin had enough world distribution that it would be recognizable to anyone with even the slightest knowledge of medicine. Whether or not the Corsicans would have some was anybody's guess.

Fayden poured his box of silver into an empty sand bag while I stuffed six C-ration box meals into another.

After dousing the cave lights, we exited and made our way back toward daylight.

It was nearing 0845 hours when Fayden and I headed out of the cave into a dismal, pelting rain. He said he thought he could make it to the Corsicans' encampment and back in six hours if he ran all the way.

I'd walked with him to the base of the rock trough and given him a wink and a thumbs-up. He smiled, then turned and jogged away into the rain-shrouded jungle.

As the wet wind lashed across my face, I felt a warming sense of admiration for his courage and loving allegiance to his son.

# Chapter 8

Howling winds meshed with cold rain whipped at my poncho like a tattered sail in a tempest as I stumbled up the rocky trough motioning my hunkered teammates to follow me to the cave.

Our new hole-in-the-wall hideout was larger than the cave we'd RON'd at last night and it had the added benefit of no animal shit.

I positioned Pug at the cave entrance to watch the approach, then distributed the C's, making sure Ski got his beans and franks. Rham asked if he could start a heat-tab fire for our meals. I rogered. We'd been in the bush three days now, eating nothing but cold LRPRs—a hot C-ration meal complete with a shared dessert of pound cake, fruit cocktail, peaches, and pears would improve everybody's spirits. It was a low-level hobo feast that the team deserved.

"Did Sunburst have traffic for us?" I asked, carving a P-38 around the rim of my C and bending the top back.

"Oh, yeah," Ski responded, reaching into his shirt pocket and taking out a small, green notebook. "They told us two things we already know. Increased Pathet-Lao activity in the Northeastern Prairie Fire AO . . . and heavy rain forecasts."

I set my C on a rock at the edge of the fire. "Nothing about Duell?"

"No. Were you expecting something?"

"Not really. Probably just my optimistic radar working overtime again."

"What op-a-mis-ic mean, Sar Brett?" Tuong interjected.

I thought for a moment trying to assemble an explanation he'd understand. "Do you remember Murphy's Law?"

He smiled. "Rog-ee. Ifing sum-ting can go wrong, it go wrong."

"Okay. Optimism is Murphy's law bass-ackwards."

"It's like P.M.A., Tuong," Ski butted in. "You know, positive mental attitude," he said while dipping his spoon back and forth from can to mouth with a mechanical cadence Dale Carnegie would have been proud of.

"Arnold! Will you ever stop trying to AI me. All it does is complicate things."

"Roger. Okay, okay, Brett."

"What AI mean?"

"It means Assistant Instructor!" I said, lifting my can away from the fire.

"Oh," Tuong responded in a soft tone indicating he'd opted not to ask what it was.

I decided it was time to change magazines on the conversation. "Tell me what you know about these Corsicans, babysan. Did you ever run into them when you were working up here with the Agency?"

"Corsicans?" Ski blurted.

"Just listen, partner. You may accidentally learn something."

"Yes, I'm see dem two time. Dae bring many ting wid dem and Jim Bee too."

My eyebrows raised. "Jim Beam? Did you say Jim Beam?"

"Rogee. Dae bring lots booze. Have party. Get dunk! Den buy ya-ying cheap."

The Corsican method of doing business didn't surprise me. It did bother me a little that they were doing some of it with my brand of liquor. "Where do these guys operate out of?" I asked, passing the community canteen-dessert-cup over to Lok.

"Ban Ban."

I took out my map, found our position, then computed the rough distance roundtrip to Ban Ban.

"That's about forty klicks!" I looked at Tuong. "How's Fayden think he's going to go there and back in six hours? . . . In a storm!"

"I'm tink no sweat. Him run and go flat lan way. No mountain," Tuong answered, moving to view my map.

Looking closer, I noticed that our mountain location above Na Dao sloped into a wide open valley that hooked northeast toward the road junction of Highway Seven and Highway Six. Ban Ban was situated at the junction of the two roads.

Fayden's route of travel would be easier than mountain trails, but considering the volume of rain and Pathet-Lao activity in the area, he'd still have a long row to hoe.

Initially, I'd thought about sending Tuong with him to act as interpreter in case Fayden ran into a language barrier. Although Tuong wasn't fluent in French he knew some, but I'd decided it wasn't fair to ask him to go out on the limb for something that was one-hundred-eighty degrees opposite our mission requirements.

Fayden had departed almost an hour ago: 0900. If he was able to travel the forty klicks, approximately twenty-five miles, in six hours that would put his ETA back here at 1500. That would give me about four hours of daylight to get to Chung's village, give them the medication, and RTC—return to cave.

My plan was to leave the team in place and take Fayden and Tuong with me to the village; I knew I'd need Tuong to explain the time interval between dosages to Chung's mother.

After returning we'd RON in place and press on with the mission at first light.

Additionally, I planned to ask Fayden to work as guide and advisor for us since he knew the area, and, as a Hmong, had a vested interest in the recovery of Duell. With Fayden as the hood ornament on RT Texas we'd have a much better chance of avoiding enemy contact.

A clatter of thunder boomed in the near distance. "Are these Corsicans armed?" I asked, glancing at the curtain of rain blowing across the cave entrance.

"Rogee. Having pis-tos."

"Why are you so interested in these French guys? Seems to me like they're friendly to the Hmong. I mean, after all, they're buying their opium," Ski said casually while digging the last remnants of dessert from the canteen cup.

"Oh, I'm sure they're friendly all right. Just as long as they're getting bargain basement prices on the best opium in the world," I said, moving toward Pug and nodding that I'd take over the guard spot.

"But there's a difference between being friendly and being friends. Major Helton told me that Abe Duell is probably the only true friend the Hmong have ever had."

"Well, how about the missionaries over here? In that briefing they said there were a few missionaries out here too."

I opened a small pack of Chicklets and popped the gum into my mouth. "The way I see it, there's only a fine line between missionaries and mercenaries. They both want something, they just go about it in different ways."

"I guess you're right, but you can't deny the fact that the Corsicans are paying money, real silver, to the people here. So, what the heck, seems fair to me."

"What these people need is knowledge, not silver. They live a hand-to-mouth existence on the edge of starvation. Duell is the one being fair; he's giving them knowledge they can use to feed their families," I said, catching a glimpse of movement. "Hand me the binoculars. They're in the side pouch on my ruck."

"You see something?"

"Maybe," I answered, leaning toward Ski.

I took the field glasses and focused on the lower approach. Through the dark screen of rain I saw the vague outline of a buck. The animal was limping slowly up the rocky path. He stopped, moved his head from side to side as if sniffing the air, then turned and moved back down the trough.

"What is it?" Ski whispered as Tuong crept nearer to me.

I lowered the glasses to my lap. "Just a deer."

"That's good," Ski said, leaning back against his ruck. "At least we know the Pathet-Lao aren't around. I mean, a deer wouldn't be in the area if there were humans around. Right?"

"Roger." I was pleased to hear that Binkowski's mind seemed to be back on track—thinking recon. ". . . But then, we're here, aren't we?" I added just to make sure Ski didn't get too lax about our position.

"You know the great thing about C-rations?" Ski asked, reaching into the brown, cellophane bag that came with the meal packet. He pulled out a small package of Winstons and answered his own question. "I mean, beside the fact that they taste better than LRPRs, they give us four cigarettes in these neat, little packs," he said cheerfully.

I wasn't on any soapbox about smoking, but my team SOP didn't allow it in the field. Although everyone on the team smoked but me, it was always Binkowski who tried to bend the rule. I knew what was coming. I kept my gaze on the rain but could see him fondling the package out of the corner of my eye.

"I guess . . . well, the time I really enjoy a cigarette most is after a good meal."

I ignored his tracer. "Did you bring that Claymore in when I pulled y'all back?"

"The Claymore? The one you told me to—"

"Yeah, that one."

"Well, ah . . . no, I didn't."

"How about going down and bringing it in. Someone might spot it down there."

"Brett! It's raining like a son-of-a-bitch out there! I can't—"

"You'll be all right, Arnold. You can have a cigarette while you're gone. Lok, let's heat some coffee water, buddy."

"Shit!" Ski muttered, yanking his poncho hood up and over his head while moving toward the opening. ". . . trying to smoke a cigarette out there would be like—like trying to eat a doughnut underwater!"

# Chapter 9

RT Texas spent the remainder of the morning and half the afternoon cleaning weapons, filling canteens, washing, and napping. I rotated our guard post each hour.

At 1500 hours I was crouched at the cave entrance peering anxiously into the droning pall of rain searching for any sign of movement.

Half an hour later Tuong nudged me out of my trance. "Sar Brett, you wan I go checkee?" he whispered, huddling near me.

I took a gulp of cold coffee and cracked a half-grin to let him know I appreciated his idea. "I'd like to, babysan, but I don't know where we'd begin to look for him." I glanced at my watch, brushing water off the crystal. "He's only thirty minutes overdue and considering he doesn't even have a watch I'd say it's too early to start biting our nails."

I set my cup aside, raised the binoculars to my eyes, and continued to study the dim path. After a while I started imagining that I was seeing things through the rain. Pulling the field glasses away I blinked several times to sooth my tired eyes.

"Brett, you said there weren't any medical supplies in that cache. That's unusual, isn't it? Are you sure you did a good search?" Binkowski asked.

"Like, remember that dead NVA you told me to search after we nailed that patrol a few weeks—"

"Yes, I remember."

"Well, I'm only sayin' this because I thought I'd searched him real good and then you went over the body and found a map and—"

"I get the picture, Ski. Yes, I'm sure I searched the—" I stopped and thought back to the moments spent looking through the rows of boxes. I hadn't opened any. I'd been looking at labels, not contents, and I'd been too hasty.

"Partner, I don't like to say so, but I'm glad you mentioned it. I didn't search it worth a damn!

"Tuong, can you lead the way through that tunnel again without tripping those booby traps?"

"Rogee, Sar Brett! No sweat."

"Good. Here . . . take my flashlight. Head back in there and check out those boxes and the crates. You know what we're looking for. Take Ski with you."

"Me! Why me?" Binkowski muttered.

"It was your idea, partner. And a damn good one!"

"Wait, Brett. I'm so big and that tunnel, it—it honestly cramps me. I'm not sure I oughta push my luck trying to—"

"You did it once. You'll be fine. There's no black cats in there. Just be careful going by that big rock."

He scowled, then glanced at the small package of Winstons lying on top of his C-ration box. Ski quickly tucked the pack into his shirt pocket and stood, radiating a defiant grin.

As Tuong and Binkowski removed the rock to enter the tunnel, I caught a glimpse of something moving low in the distance. I focused the binoculars. It was Fayden, crawling.

"Hold up! He's back!" I shouted, grabbing my rifle. I jumped to my feet and bolted out into the rain with Pug following.

Rain-splattered blood oozed from scratches and cuts

streaked across Fayden's body. His hand gripped the leather strap of his empty arrow quiver. No crossbow. I threw my rifle to Pug, and lifted the Hmong, cradling him in my arms.

I stumbled hurriedly back to the cave. "Phan, Lok, spread out that poncho!" I said, crouching as I entered. "Ski, give me that liner!"

I knelt, placing him on the poncho, then began wiping the liner over his body to clear away the water and blood. Fayden was partially coherent but exhausted and nearly hyperthermal. He trembled and mumbled weakly as my fingers scanned his body searching for bullet holes and gashes. None.

"What the fuck happened to him?"

"Looks like claw marks," I said, glancing at Ski. "There's a towel in my ruck. Get it. Then pass me my aid kit."

Tuong knelt at my side as I folded the poncho liner and tucked it under Fayden's head.

"I'll bet anything he got attacked, attacked by a tiger or something," Ski said, handing the towel to me.

"Maybe. What do you think, babysan?"

"Not tiger. Maybe ape. Where crossbow?"

"Didn't have it. All he had was this," I answered, pulling the leather quiver strap gently from Fayden's grasp.

His grip tightened as his head jerked abruptly forward. "Ampa-silly, Ampa—Ampa—" he mumbled lethargically.

"Take it easy, partner," I said, loosening my grip on his hand and coaxing him to lean his head back.

Fayden had obviously been attacked by something. His body was half covered with superficial scratches, but they looked more like the common house-cat type rather than tiger claw marks. I dried and treated the cuts with antiseptic, then blotched his body with Band-aids and gauze patches. I'd decided that right now he needed rest more than food. We covered him with a poncho liner and let him sleep.

Tuong dropped a heat tab in an empty can and lit it. "Look like back square one, Sar Brett," he said, giving me a somber glance.

I ignored it. Ski didn't.

"Look at the bright side," Binkowski chirped. "At least he's still alive."

"Pour some coffee water. I don't need a fucking pep talk, Ski," I said, taking another poncho liner and covering Fayden's body. "I'll monitor him for a few minutes, then we're going into that cache and run a finetooth comb through every box and crate."

"Brett, you know, this is turning into a career effort. What happens if we don't find any Ampicillin. I hate to say it but—"

"Then don't say it, Arnold!" I parried.

"Sar Brett, I'm tink sum-ting dinky-dow," Tuong broke in while frowning at Fayden.

"What?"

"Him no have crossbow. No arrow, but have here." He touched the empty, leather quiver that the Hmong still held at his side.

Ski leaned to look over us. "That's not weird. Obviously whatever jumped him caused him to lose his crossbow and the quiver was all he escaped with. Simple."

"Not so fast, Watson," I said, easing the quiver strap out of Fayden's hand. I raised the empty, cylindrical container to peer inside.

Seeing nothing, I inverted the arrow scabbard and tapped it against my palm. "There's something in here, but . . . Phan give me that cleaning rod."

Pushing the rod down inside the quiver, I felt something spongy at the bottom. Prying, pushing, and pulling the rod back and forth I dislodged several wet lumps of paper which were stuffed inside. I tossed the wadded paper aside and tilted the quiver toward my open hand. A small brown bottle dropped into my palm like a big gold nugget on an assayer's scale. "Out-fuckin'-standing," I shouted, holding the bottle closer to study the small, printed label. It read:

POLYCILLIN (AMPICILLIN)
500 mg.
BRISTOL MFG. U.S.A.
USE ONLY AS PRESCRIBED

"Shit! This is good, ole U.S.A. medicine. Tuong, if I was queer I'd kiss ya!"

"No for me!" Tuong snapped, jumping back. "What is da?"

"Get your poncho on, babysan. We go now!" I said, stuffing the bottle in my pocket and glancing at my watch. "It's 1620 hours, Ski. We'll be back by 1930. When Fayden wakes up tell him he's great! Tell him Tuong and I have gone to his village. Tell him to stay put and give him a hot C-rat meal."

"But—but . . . wait, I've got questions. What if—"

I grabbed his shoulder and grinned. "You're in charge, partner. If you got questions, you answer them."

"Tuong, let's *dee*."

Leaving our rucks with the team, Tuong and I moved outside into stinging rain and made our way slowly back down toward the trail that Fayden had brought us out on.

After reaching the path and moving beneath the canopy we were shielded from the pelting rain. I put Tuong in the lead slot and told him to set a double-time pace. As we jogged along the dim, dripping corridor I was well aware that we were violating the first cardinal rule of recon— never take the same trail in that you took coming out.

# Chapter 10

With Tuong on point, I had one of the best bush sensors in the business of jungle warfare. He knew the smells and sounds that belonged here and the ones that didn't. Some months back, while working point, he'd saved us from an NVA meat-grinder ambush by actually smelling a *nuc-mom* fart. Later, he admitted that if the wind hadn't been directly in our face he would never have detected the ambush until the first rounds ripped through him.

Two hundred meters into our trek, Tuong stopped just ahead of me, then turned and doubled back behind me. I watched as he squatted to examine the path surface, scanning his fingers over the wet humus as if reading Braille.

"What's up?" I whispered.

He stood. "Looksee, make sure we no leave tak. Is okay," he replied without the slightest hint of labored breath.

We pressed on for another fifteen fast-paced minutes until reaching a sharp bend in the path. Tuong arm-signaled me to stop. He turned, touched his eyes, and pointed forward, then he slowly moved ahead to examine the lead section of trail.

I knelt and waited, estimating we'd traveled over half the distance to Fayden's village. Although I hadn't been able to ask Fayden, I was reasonably certain the trail led to the village. I took out my map, shielding it with my hand while I studied our position. It didn't surprise me that the trail wasn't depicted on the map. Using a grease pencil I noted the approximate countour of the trail.

We were halted in the zone where we'd encountered the Pat patrol earlier this morning.

Tucking the map away, I peered back down the trail, then eased forward trying to view Tuong. Low limbs sagged across the dim path, swaying gently like a ragged curtain on an outdoor stage.

Tuong hurried toward me. Upon reaching my position he held out his hand showing me two 7.62 expended brass cartridges. They had been fired recently as evidenced by the lack of oxidization.

Tuong read my eyes and shrugged. "Me no hear nothing."

"What's the trail like up there?"

He turned and extended his arm straight. "Long. Berry stray. Not good."

I decided not to waste time standing around trying to guess why there was recently expended brass on the trail. I also decided not to push our luck any further by continuing on a straight path.

I withdrew my compass, took an azimuth and motioned for Tuong to head us off the trail.

By 1710 hours we'd clawed and excavated our way through the thickest rain forest I'd ever encountered during twelve months running Prairie Fire targets. The good news was, we'd stayed on azimuth. I'd been the self-inflicted dupe of taking easy-route land navigation before.

After locating the woodpile area near the east side of the village, we rested. I wrapped a fresh cravat around a cut on my arm that Tuong pointed out to me. I hadn't even felt the cut until he brought it to my attention.

I slipped my poncho hood off and leaned back, turning my face up into the cold rain. Combing my fingers through wet hair, I tilted forward and winked at Tuong. "Partner, did I ever tell you you're exceptional? In fact, so are Lok, Phan, and Pug.''

"What mean x-cep-n-al?"

"Same same, out-fucking-standing," I said, pushing upward on my rifle to stand.

"Me op-a-mis-ic too!"

"Me too. Now let's go make a house call on Chung."

We skirted the tree line around the woodpile area, then moved across a brush-covered knoll that bounded the east side of the village.

A muffled chorus of barking dogs resounded in the distance, briefly obscured by a sudden rumble of thunder. Tuong knelt at the berm just ahead of me, studying the rain-masked village twenty meters ahead.

I knelt at Tuong's side, glanced to the rear, then peered toward the quiet silhouette of huts. No sign of movement.

We stood and walked abreast, rifles leveled. Nearing the first hut Tuong crouched, veering left. I followed, staying off to his right side, feeling the mud suck at my boots.

Tuong halted, uttering something as his rifle slowly lowered.

"What'd you say?" I whispered, moving forward.

"Pat-Lao come dis place," he answered with a hard frown.

My stunned eyes narrowed and stared toward a lumped pile of bodies sprawled in front of the Shaman's hooch. "What the hell!" I mumbled, squinting at the pack of dogs feeding on the carnage.

I ran forward waving my arms, scattering the mongrels. My eyes darted glances across the corpse-splotched village as I stumbled madly toward Chung's hooch. Ripping the door flap aside I lurched into the stench of point-blank horror.

Bullet riddled and blood soaked, the little boy lay contorted into a fetal position. The stump of his frail arm still hung suspended as I'd tied it. Dropping to my knees, I leaned, fanning away the droning mass of flies, wanting to caress his dark, matted hair. My hands trembled fumbling to untie the cord and gently lower his arm. I turned away trying to halt my tears, then saw the naked buttocks of his mother. She was bent forward over a small barrel as if the butcher had raped her from the rear, then shot her in the head as she endured his heathen thrust. In the blinding moment of rage I wondered if Chung had been forced to witness the savage ritual of his mother's rape and execution.

A burst of fire rent the air. I whirled, jerking my rifle toward the door, falling into a prone firing position. Crawling to the muddy mouth of the doorway, I peered out into the rainy dusk.

"No shoot! It me, Sar Brett!" Tuong shouted, trudging into my sights.

"What the fuck! What were you firing at?"

"I shoot focking dog try eat there," he said, pointing emphatically at a dead little girl sprawled out front. The bloody carcass of a dog lay in the same faded crimson puddle.

"Is the village clear?" I asked, raising to my knees.

"Rogee. I'm checkee. I'm also tink Pat-Lao we see befo same same do here," he said, moving his arm and pointing at the macabre human wasteland.

Standing, I saw a chicken pecking at the bloody face of an infant. Leveling my CAR-15, I triggered a quick burst, scattering chicken guts and feathers through the bleak shroud of drizzle.

Lowering my head I took a deep breath. "How fucking long since they were here?"

"I'm tink maybe two hour."

"Why—why did they have do this? These people weren't any threat to them! Why?" I shouted.

Tuong glanced shyly at the doorway, then stepped forward to look inside. "Dat why," he said, staring at the bodies.

I blinked. "What? . . . That little boy couldn't be—"

"I see befo. Pat-Lao come where American help Hmong. No like. Kill all."

"You—you mean because I fuckin' helped him they killed, cut down this whole goddamn village? Simply be . . . because—"

"VC do same to Montagnards, Vietnam."

I slumped against the door of the hooch feeling the heavy chill of rain, regret, and defeat. I knew about the ruthless tortures and mass slaughters the VC and NVA inflicted on the Montagnards—this was the first time my eyes had been stabbed with the vision of it in Laos.

"Move through here and check to see if anyone is alive."

"I'm already do. All *fini*."

"All right. Head down to the trail entrance and wait for me. I'll be there in a minute. And keep a sharp eye, partner. The bastards may know we're in the area."

As Tuong moved away, I turned and gripped the door cover, ripping it loose. I walked slowly into the hut and knelt at Chung's body. I laid the canvas over the little boy trying not to cry as I gently tucked the edges of cloth under him.

My voice quivered as I touched him and relented to the aching flow of tears. "Your suffering is over, young warrior, but I promise you this. They will pay! These mountains will flow with Communist blood before I leave . . . before I leave."

As I exited Chung's hooch into a dimming veil of drizzle, I saw Tuong approaching followed by four indigenous soldiers. The men wore American-style fatigues and carried M-16 rifles but no backpacks. I kept my weapon leveled. The appearance of their rifles at shoulder arms told me they weren't hostile.

"Sar Brett, these men Vang Pao patro. Come search for Tan-Pop," Tuong announced, glancing around at the stout man nearest him. "Dis man name Ha. Him, Sar Yon-cee."

Ha ignored the introduction. His hard eyes traveled slowly over the carnage. He quickly muttered some orders to the other men while pointing at the pile of bodies in front of the Shaman's hut.

"How'd they know about this massacre?" I asked Tuong while lowering my CAR-15 and giving a perfunctory nod to Ha.

"Dae meet old man who run from village tell Pat-Lao come here."

It was apparent that Vang Pao had long-range patrols working the area in the hunt for Duell but I'd received no intel report on it.

Some of Ha's men began dragging bodies into the huts with all the reverent ceremony of a common police-call. I figured their apathy was a result of having done it many times.

"Hold it!" I snapped, stepping abruptly in front of a man about to enter Chung's hut. "Tuong, tell him I'll take care of this."

Ha peered beyond me with slitted eyes studying the hut interior as Tuong spoke, then he directed the soldier to check another hooch.

Looking back, Ha gave me a grin that was missing several front teeth. "You Cee-Cee-N!" he blurted.

My eyebrows raised involuntarily hearing the term CCN. "That's right," I answered accepting his Americanized version of a jolting handshake. "You speak English."

"Lee-tol bit Englee only. I learn from sum Spec-shol-Fors sna-bite teem work here sum."

Ha's knowledge of Special Forces operations ran deeper than the law allowed; Snake-bite teams were top secret and then some. They launched out of the First Special Forces Group on Okinawa. Although SBT's were comprised of six personnel like C and C, that was where the similarity ended. The One-Zero and One-One were usu-

ally Spanish or Oriental. The indigenous team members
were generally former NVA, captured or surrendered, and
liked the idea of making big bucks working for us. SBT's
wore NVA uniforms and carried AKs—they could move
right into Chuck's safe areas, smile, and blow them away
before the NVA could say, "Costume Party."

I needed to know if there was a SBT in on the hunt for
Duell. Taking a pack of C-ration Marlboros from my
pocket I handed it to Ha along with a question. "Snake-
bite here now?" I asked as he smiled and opened the
pack.

Ha looked at me curiously, then stepped beneath the
eaves of the hooch to light a cigarette.

I glanced at Tuong, then waited while Ha pondered his
first draw of the smoke. My concern about the presence
of an "Okie" SBT in the AO was a simple precaution to
make sure I took a second look before I ambushed them
by mistake. In the days ahead I planned to "lead-shred"
anything and everything that resembled a scum-sucking
communist.

The drizzle began to fade with the twilight. It seemed
Ha was ignoring my question; just when I started to reit-
erate it he spoke. "Why you not know if sna-bite teem
here?" he asked, grinning, as if he enjoyed knowing
something that I didn't.

Some conversational techniques were evidently international—snaggletooth was trying to answer a question
with a question. I decided not to play interrogatory Ping-
Pong. My question could be answered during my next radio contact.

"Doesn't matter!" I said, ignoring him and looking at
my watch: 1815. "I've got something that needs to be
done right now. Tuong, how about talking with this gent
and finding out what you can about what's going on in this
area. And ask him if he's got a line on Tan-Pop. We need
to *dee* in about thirty minutes."

Tuong nodded. "Rogee, Sar Brett."

"Ho!" Ha exclaimed, as I started to turn and move into the hooch. "Where you teem?"

I smirked, and answered using Ha's own idiom. "Why you not know?"

After wrapping and tying the little boy's body, I exited the hooch and carried him to the tree where the Shaman indicated they would bury Chung's arm.

Using my rifle stock I dug into the soft mud and found the leaf-wrapped residue of the arm. I placed it near Chung and began clawing deeper into the soft earth until I'd dug a four-foot grave for his body. I gently placed Chung into the grave, then positioned the arm by him and carefully scooped handfuls of dirt and mud over him until the grave was filled and well-packed.

Reaching a muddy hand to my neck, I yanked away a gold chain with a Buddha pendant that Tuong had given me months ago. I dug a small depression in the grave, placed the stone-carved Buddha into it, and caked mud over it. I moved over and sat with my back pressed against the tree.

Removing my bush hat, I placed it over the muzzle of my rifle and took an anguished breath. I stared in silence, first at the dark, cloud-blotched sky, then slowly back to the muddy mound of earth at my feet.

My jaw clinched, fighting—denying—tears, until finally I spoke quietly. "We—we never got a chance to talk much, Chung, but I believe you're probably the bravest young warrior I've ever known. I wish I could have known you longer. And I wish, if my little boy could have lived, that he could have been your friend too. I'll—I'll bet you could have taught him how to shoot a crossbow . . . and well . . . maybe he—he could have taught you how—how to play baseball and—and—and . . . goddammit, those pukes will pay for this! They'll . . . pay—pay with every drop of blood I can choke out of—"

"Sar Brett," a voice intruded.

"What!" I shouted, darting an eye toward the voice.

Tuong moved closer. "Maybe we nee go. Ha, him say many Pat-Lao come soon."

I stood slowly and slapped my bush hat against my leg. I slipped my rifle sling over my neck and peered at Tuong. "Many Pathet-Lao come; is that what you said?"

"Yes. Ha say soon. Tonigh maybe."

"That's great," I said softly. "That's great. Because they're coming to die."

# Chapter 11

It was almost 1900 hours when Tuong and I bid Ha and his team farewell and set out, using a route back to the cache that Ha recommended. The route was an old, partially overgrown path which wove through several abandoned corn fields. Although it hooked about a mile off the more direct course, it was worth the extra distance considering we were now traveling at night and more rain appeared imminent.

Prior to leaving, Ha made it a point to let me know that a Snake-bite team was working the northern edge of our AO. He didn't know what their mission was, but he said they'd been on the ground one day and were moving toward an NVA training and maintenance facility north of Ban Ban. When I asked if he knew the team name, Ha replied, "Anny-coda." I knew the team leader of RT Anaconda, Jim Cortez, from a previous joint mission I'd been part of when working as Swede Jensen's One-One on RT California. Jim was considered a "wire tap" mission specialist. I wasn't sure, but it was my WAG that he was headed in to plant a listening device at the NVA facility.

When I'd asked Ha if he'd ever seen any Pathet-Lao wearing a French-style Havelock cap, he replied, after I sketched a picture of it, "No." I told him that I felt it was Havelock Harry and his heathen quartet that massacred the village and that they were now on my most-wanted list. Ha had nodded grimly, then told me to avoid Na Dao, saying that his intel net indicated a build-up of Pats moving in to occupy the village. I smiled and thanked him.

Tuong kept a quick pace as we traversed an inclined, open area on the side of a mountain. The night winds lapped hard at my poncho, blowing it upward like a hoop-skirted dress. When we reached the other side of the clearing, a deep, piercing growl stopped us dead in our tracks. It was so close, my sphincter slammed shut like a rifle bolt. I quickly flipped my selector to full auto.

"Tiger," Tuong whispered, pointing into the pitch-black forest ahead.

"No shit," I answered. "Let's move away some, baby-san."

I didn't like the idea of taking on a Bengal tiger in broad daylight—night was out of the fucking question. Backing carefully away, I felt a cool breath of wind roll over my neck. "Easy partner, he's getting a nose full of us right now," I said, tensing my trigger finger. My eyes traveled in line with the muzzle of my weapon as I scanned the dark tangles of the tree line.

As we withdrew slowly toward the center of the small field, I glanced at Tuong. "We're too close, partner," I uttered while angling my movement away from him to put some distance between us.

Suddenly, as if catapulted out of hell, a massive creature hurled toward me like a missile. My finger welded to the trigger, spitting a savage stream of point-blank lead at the beast. Recoil—muzzle flashes—racket, jolted my adrenalin as the unyielding beast sprang high for the kill. Thrusting my rifle upward I hammered more lead into the creature, then felt the chamber empty. Diving away, I rolled madly and yanked the knife from my shoulder scabbard.

Clawing mud, I struggled to rise up on my knees, then

heard a blaring burst of automatic fire. "*Fini*! Sar Brett, *fini*! You okay? You okay?"

"O-okay," I muttered. My eyes found Tuong in the quiet darkness. He strode slowly toward the sprawled tiger, keeping his weapon aimed on the still animal.

Standing, I gulped several breaths, then stumbled ahead to see the vague, striped outline of the long Bengal stretched in front of Tuong. With the front and rear legs extended it easily spanned ten feet.

"*Beaucoup* tiger," Tuong said softly.

"That's strange," I mumbled. "A minute ago it looked like a damn bull-elephant!" I slid my knife into the scabbard and snapped the retainer strap. "Help me find my rifle, quick-draw. We gotta get the hell out of here before his big brother gets here."

After locating and dislodging my CAR-15 from beneath the tiger, I quickly wiped the weapon off and reloaded. As Tuong and I moved on into the night I sensed what felt like a wad of paste car wax rubbing along the crack of my ass.

It was past 2000 hours when Tuong and I neared base camp hole-in-the-wall. In his route recommendation, Ha had neglected to inform us about a fork in the old trail— we traveled almost a mile out of our way before realizing that we'd taken the wrong turn. The wrong turn had two tactical benefits: it led to a southerly flowing river that was not depicted on my map, and it oriented us to another uncharted trail. It was beginning to dawn on me that the only similarity between my map and the AO was the color green.

When Tuong and I moved back up the trough to re-enter the cave, I silently added two gold stars to Binkowski's leadership progress chart—Ski had initiated and positioned himself and Pug on LP, and he used a challenge as we approached.

"We were expecting you over thirty minutes ago. What

kept you?'' Ski whispered while sniffing me as I crouched near him. ''You smell like—''

''Never mind that. How's Fayden doing?''

''He's awake but still kinda shaky. He's sorta irritated at me, I think, because he wanted to go and follow you and I told him to stay put like you said. And well, I'm sure he'll get over it. How's Chung?''

A chill rippled through me. I stood and peered into the blank face of wind not wanting to admit to reality.

''Brett, Brett, did you hear me? I—''

''He's dead! He was slaughtered . . . the whole village was slaughtered.''

''What?'' Ski blurted, standing. ''That's not . . . fun—''

''That's right,'' I said, turning and staring at the dark profile of his face. ''It's not funny. It's—it's just the fucking truth.''

''You mean, you mean everybody, all those kids and—''

''Everybody! The women, little kids, babies, old men, all cut down by the brave Pathet-Lao.''

''But—but . . . I . . . why?'' Ski sighed and asked.

''Tyranny doesn't need any goddamn reason why. Fucking heathens only understand one thing. They only respect one thing!'' I stepped closer to Binkowski, holding my weapon to his face. ''Firepower,'' I whispered. ''Firepower.''

I paused, took a deep breath, then lowered my rifle. ''We'll be changing our RON tonight. You stay in position for now and I'll send Phan down to relieve you in a while,'' I said, turning and motioning for Tuong to follow me.

''Where . . . what are you gonna do?''

''I've got to tell Fayden about his village . . . about his family, and about something called recoil-retribution.''

The burden I felt in my heart made the twenty-meter walk up to the cave the longest emotional stretch I'd ever had to travel. Fayden was squatted beside Lok at the cave mouth when we approached. After moving inside, I hung my poncho over the entrance and lit a heat tab to provide some low light—I wanted Fayden to see my eyes as we unfolded the story.

Fayden greeted us, smiling and talking enthusiastically to Tuong. I didn't have to inquire about what he was asking. Tuong looked at me, awaiting my signal before speaking.

I sat down, removed my bush hat, and glanced at Tuong. "Go ahead, partner, tell him about it. But, don't . . . there's no need to tell him about what they did to his wife."

I watched as Fayden squatted near Tuong and listened. When Tuong finished, the solemn-faced Hmong slowly tilted his head and gazed down at the blue flame dancing in the can. Strangely, I remembered part of a psychology professor's class lecture about the phases of grief: "The first phase of grief is denial," he'd said. There was no evidence of denial on Fayden's face. Outwardly he seemed to accept the harsh reality as if it was part of the cruel way of life here, but I knew it was twisting him apart inside.

I remembered more about the psych class. According to the textbooks, there were five phases of grief, the fifth being acceptance. It was a neatly wrapped academic package with a tidy explanation all geared for domestic application. But here and now I was about to add sub-paragraph "A" to the fifth phase of grief and I planned to call it "payback."

Fayden raised his head slowly and stared at the dim reflection of light on the cave wall. A tear made its way down his cheek. My jaw tightened, hearing only the lonely howl of night wind whispering through my tattered poncho.

I searched my mind for something to help comfort him. Finally, I turned and said, "Tuong, tell him that it is my promise that I will find and kill the bastards that did it."

Tuong paused, then looked over at me. "I'm already tell him, Sar Brett."

I blinked. "How did you know?"

"Becau, I'm—I'm know how you tink."

Fayden brushed away his tears and spoke slowly while casting alternating glances at Tuong and me. Tuong told me the Hmong said he must leave and go to his village.

I nodded and told Fayden where I'd buried his son and mentioned that a Hmong patrol led by a man named Ha had conducted the burial of his wife and the other villagers. I then asked Tuong to urge him not to go to the village tonight, saying that if he would wait until morning we'd go with him. Fayden declined.

Breathing a heavy sigh of anguish, I 'looked back. "Okay, Tuong, tell him that I understand his need. Tell him that the Pathet-Lao I'm looking for, the ones that hit his village, were led by a Lao wearing an old style French cap. You know, the type with the flap, the cloth that hangs down in back.

"And tell him that I'm going to need his help to find them."

Fayden nodded grimly as Tuong interpreted my words. Then I reached into my pocket and withdrew his wife's silver necklace. I'd uncovered it from her hiding place prior to leaving the village.

Fayden's eyes glistened as I wrapped the necklace back into the black scarf and handed it to him. He slowly stood and spoke while walking over to the tunnel entrance. Tuong explained that before returning to his village, Fayden was going to enter the cache and store his wife's treasure in the same hole where he'd kept their silver.

I set my rifle aside and began removing my web gear. "We'll go with him."

"Why we go, Sar Brett?"

"Because we have some shopping to do, partner."

Less than an hour later, Tuong, Fayden, and I returned

from the cache supermarket with four LAWs, six Claymores, and five AK-47s with magazine vests and ammo.

As we stacked the gear, I could tell that Fayden was anxious to leave and return to his village. After determining that he was proficient in the use of an AK-47, I convinced him to take one just in case he ran into the Pathet-Lao we were looking for. I didn't necessarily anticipate that Havelock Harry and gang would be in the area, but if they were, I at least wanted Fayden to have a fighting chance.

Prior to his departure, I made sure that he understood where I planned to RON—I told him we would be a stone's throw south of the old trail that split where it met the river. He acknowledged that he knew the area and said he would join us by first light.

When Fayden left, I sent Lok to pull Binkowski and Pug back to the cave before we moved out to our new RON site. While waiting, I mentally tallied the combined firepower we now had. Our standard munitions load required each man to carry twenty-four magazines of 5.56, two Claymores, and eight M-26 frag grenades. With the extra Claymores, LAWs, and AKs, we were now officially qualified as "loaded for bear."

When Ski, Pug, and Phan returned to the cave, I lit another heat tab for light and distributed the additional armament to the team. I gave each of the Cowboys an AK and full magazine vest, telling them to wear the vest loosely over their web gear. I told them that Ski and I would carry their CARs during tactical movement. I also told them to stash their bush hats and wear cravats, rolled bandanna style around their foreheads.

After passing Ski two of the LAWs and another three Claymores, he gave me a dejected look like he'd been given the wrong toys on Christmas morning. "Well, hey . . . how come I don't get to carry an AK? You know I'm qualified with the AK too."

"Arnold," I said, opening the flap on my ruck. "Have you ever heard of Snake-bite teams?"

"Well, sure. They're the ones that dress up like NVA."

"That's right. I'm putting the Cowboys out front to lure any enemy we happen to cross. I hate to disappoint you, but at six-foot-four, you'd never make it as an NVA decoy, buddy. We're not going to win the door prize at the costume party, but from a distance the Cowboys will look like Pathet-Lao."

"Now you understan, Skee?" Tuong chided.

"Do you know anything about firing a LAW?" I asked quickly.

"Roger. I fired one in basic training. It's simple, but these things are meant for tanks. There aren't any tanks around here."

Placing the Claymores inside my ruck, I remembered the Special Forces camp at Lang Vei that got overrun by Soviet PT-76 tanks. "No tanks around here," I repeated. "You know that's what the generals said about Lang Vei, Arnold."

# Chapter 12

It was 2310 hours when we moved out of the cave into a thick, windy drizzle. I made sure we had sterilized the area and cleared all evidence of our presence in the cave, including boot tracks.

I put Tuong on point and told him to take us to the river location we'd inadvertently discovered earlier where we'd RON. Tuong hadn't asked what pace to set and I'd decided to allow his own tactical judgment to determine how fast we'd move.

When I'd distributed the additional armament to the team, no one had asked why we were taking on more munitions on a mission that was supposed to avoid contact. It didn't surprise me that the Cowboys hadn't asked anything, but the absence of curiosity on Ski's part was unusual; I anticipated that eventually he'd hit me with a question about it.

Tuong moved us swiftly down the dark corridor as if he didn't have the least concern for any potential Pathet-Lao ambushes. His judgment coincided with my knowledge of Pathet-Lao tactics. Commonly, Pats were lazy. They would only go out on a limb when they knew they had a big advantage or when their more disciplined cousins, the NVA, were there and kicking them in the ass to get them motivated. Thus far, there had been no indication of NVA in the area, but that would likely change. My plan was to slay any and all Pathet-Lao we encountered in our area of interest—I knew that the chances were good that Havelock Harry would be among them. Then, we'd head north toward Ban Ban, make a perfunctory search for Duell, and request exfiltration.

My unadmitted feeling was that Duell was either dead or had been captured and moved north to Hanoi to use as prisoner clout along with other American POWs. The piece of the puzzle that had bothered me from the beginning was why a non-combatant, middle-aged farmer, who didn't even carry a weapon, had been a focal point of communist interest. I knew it was possible that the CIA wasn't telling me the truth about the scenario, and I knew that the agency had a habit of eliminating anyone who became a problem. But I'd read the agent's eyes clearly during the briefing when he'd said "Duell been the best source of reliable intelligence on NVA activity we've got in that neck of the woods." It seemed apparent that the CIA wanted Duell alive.

As we strode rapidly onward through the wet, slapping foliage, I reminded myself of the horror the Pats had unleashed on Chung and his mother. RT Texas had been hanging its ass out playing sneak-and-peak for four days— now it was time to switch frequencies to ambush-and-annihilate.

Soon, the gradual descent of the path indicated we were nearing the river. Minutes later, Tuong halted the team. I moved forward, tapping Pug, indicating for him to follow me. When we reached Tuong, I instructed him and Pug to evaluate the near side of the river bank and find a suitable RON site.

"Leave rucks here," I whispered. My two scouts removed their rucksacks and moved stealthily onward toward the muffled, rushing flow of water.

A succession of what sounded like Arc Light explosions

rumbled in the distance as I signaled Lok and Phan to move back up the trail and take up vigil.

"I—I can hear water," Ski whispered through a hurried breath. "Is everything okay?"

"Roger," I replied softly. "You move over there, partner. Pug and Tuong are down there checking out a spot. They'll be back in a minute."

"Roger. By the way, do—do you know if there's a full moon tonight? You know strange things happen during—"

"Dammit, Arnold, don't start that shit again! Go," I whispered emphatically. It bothered me that Ski was still obsessed with superstition.

The thick, monsoon cloud cover had prevented any lunar penetration for the past several nights, although our weather briefing had forecast a full moon in mid-November along with heavy rain. The cloud cover and rain were beneficial to clandestine movement, but rain always played tricks on Claymore hand-detonation generators.

My ambush tactic was to employ Claymore mines along a trail and blow them in series—I made a silent note to remember to wrap the generators in plastic to limit the possibility of water or moisture getting into the circuitry. It was Swede Jensen who'd taught me to wrap the hand generators: "There's nothing worse than springing a trap and suddenly realizing there ain't no snap," he'd said.

Moments later Tuong crawled through the darkness. "Sar Brett, we find pla wid good cover, but I'm have tell bad new I'm tink."

"What bad news?" I asked, edging closer to his face.

"I'm hear tiger. Rham hear too."

"Are your sure it was a tiger?"

"It not cock-a-too, Sar Brett."

"Well fuck! One damn tiger a night is all my pants can handle," I muttered under my breath. "You got any suggestions?"

"Rogee. I tink we slee berry clo, maybe okay."

Tuong's recommendation of sleeping close didn't console me much. Ordinarily, in a field RON position we slept in a wheel spoke configuration with our heads at the center. Each man maintained a one-hour sitting-up sentry, then woke the adjacent man to continue the watch. The method worked well in detecting enemy probes, but tigers were a different story and I'd already learned the hard way how incredibly quick they could be.

As heavy rain began to penetrate the canopy, I thought about my immediate options. Crossing the river was the first choice that came to mind, but I hadn't been able to determine the depth or current flow—I couldn't risk losing someone in the darkness. By returning to the cave we ran the risk of being ambushed, and moving to another location in the area gave no assurance that the predator wouldn't follow us now that he had our scent.

I'd learned that tigers were not innate man-eaters, but once they'd fed on carnage, particularly in war environments, they developed an insatiable taste for human flesh. I didn't like the idea of being on the menu.

"Sar Brett, maybe I'm having sum-ting help," Tuong said softly.

"What?"

"One time my village hab tiger come clo and my papasan say smoke keep tiger away."

"Well, did it work?"

"Work good. Everbody smoke *beaucoup* tiger go way."

I thought about it for a second. I knew the heavy rain would provide a buffer to prevent the smoke from traveling too far—that would limit the possibility of enemy detection while hopefully keeping our latest tiger deterred from the immediate area. "Do you have any cigarettes?" I asked, knowing full well it was a violation of team SOP to carry them to the field.

"No. I'm give to Skee."

"Binkowski!" I whispered loudly. "Over here."

"What's up?" Ski asked, crawling through the wet darkness.

"How many cigarettes do you have?"

"Well . . . ah gosh, I ah—"

"Don't beat around the bush. How many?"

Binkowski informed me that each of the Yards had given him their C-ration packs. "Four times four," he muttered. "That's sixteen. That's what I've got. Oh, plus I still have a couple from my pack."

I didn't have to ask what happened to Ski's other two cigarettes. He'd obviously smoked while Tuong and I had gone to the village. "Okay, partner, that's about eighteen cigarettes. Tonight we smoke and I want you to blow that stuff like a chimney."

"What? But, isn't that against—"

"Yes it is, and it's not going to get into the habit category."

After explaining the situation to Ski, we moved cautiously into our RON, set out our Claymore defense, and lit the smoking lamp. Binkowski was so elated, he volunteered for first watch.

I knew eighteen cigarettes would not get us through the entire night, but it would give us all several hours of sleep time. I instructed the team to light each successive cigarette off the stub of the last one to prevent a match flash every time a new one had to be lit.

Although I'd explained to Ski that we had a tiger in the area I decided not to tell him about the kill I'd made earlier, reasoning that Ski didn't need any supplemental fuel for his full moon theory.

Before lying back into my wagon wheel slot I handed Ski an empty, plastic, radio battery sack. "Cover those Claymore clackers with this. I don't want any malfunctions if we get hit tonight."

"Roger," he replied. "Do you want me to send a sitrep?"

"Negative. That can wait 'til morning. You just enjoy your smoke and keep your rifle tuned to rock and roll, partner."

# Chapter 13

The pale, first light of morning crept through the dripping tangles of vines and branches. It had rained heavily throughout the night, and although the downpour let up some, I could hear and feel the splatter of drops against my poncho.

At 0525 hours I woke the team and held stand-to for fifteen minutes, then sent Pug and Lok to make a circular recon of the zone. I told them to look for Fayden while they were out.

Tuong squatted near me and watched as I kac-coded our position and prepared a short message for my 0600 transmission.

"Looks like your smoke idea worked, babysan," I said, glancing at Tuong. He grinned, then gazed into the surrounding bush as if meditating.

"Ski, get the radio set up. Use the long antenna."

Ski nodded sleepily and began fitting the jointed sections of the antenna together, weaving the extended length upward through the vines.

When he'd prepared the radio, I handed him the message. "You make the contact, partner. You got four minutes 'til 0600. Tuong, when Rham and Lok get back, how about you and Phan going down and checking out that river. Head south about fifty meters, and if you can, try to find a shallow place for crossing.''

"Rogee, Sar Brett," he answered while carefully tucking his poncho liner into his rucksack.

Quick movement caught my eye. It was Lok rushing through the thicket toward us. "Pat-Lao . . . come," he whispered through labored breaths while pointing back toward our entry route.

Grabbing my rifle, I stood. "How many?"

*"Bon,"* he answered, jabbing four fingers at me. "Pug stay watch."

"Ski, Phan, Tuong, hang tight. I'm going with Lok. If we're not back in thirty minutes y'all move fifty meters downriver and wait," I said, slinging my web gear on. "Keep the Claymores in position 'til you move. Strict challenge and reply, gents!"

"Roger, Brett."

"Let's go, Lok."

I followed Lok's rapid pace through the wet thicket, feeling the tense rush of adrenalin pumping my senses to full alert. I'd split the team to cut down on noise while hurrying back to Pug. If it was only four Pats we could handle them with a hasty ambush—if it turned out to be a larger element, I'd have to wait and plan a bigger event for them.

The fact that a Pathet-Lao patrol was using the old trail indicated they were stalking us. Somewhere between the discovery of my operation on Chung and the tiger-kill gunfire last night, they'd become well-keyed to our presence. Now it was just a matter of the tried and tested recon philosophy, "He who fucks up first, fucks up last."

Crouching, Lok slowed and leveled his AK. In the dim, distant undergrowth I could see a section of the path. Suddenly, the clatter of weapons fire resonated through the jungle. We dived into prone position. Then, silence.

I edged closer to Lok. He pointed to the right, then whispered, "It come from dare. I'm leave Rham over dare,'' he said, pointing left and giving me a puzzled glance.

"You go check on Pug. I'm going to move there," I said softly, pointing in the direction of the weapons fire. "Get him and come to me."

"Rogee," he answered, moving away.

Crawling, I made my way through the foliage to the near side of the path and looked around, trying to see evidence of movement in the dripping haze. Nothing.

I stood, tensing my trigger finger, and stepped onto the path. The gunfire we'd heard had been brief, maybe twenty rounds. It had sounded like a one-sided firefight, but there was no mistaking that it was AK fire. If it had been the Pats shooting there should have been a louder chorus of racket.

As I crept to a bend in the trail, I saw a man squatted beside a body. I raised my rifle, taking aim as I moved closer. The man seemed to be talking to the body. Now, I could see several contorted figures strewn along the short span of trail.

A step closer I lowered my rifle—it was Fayden squatted and muttering to one of his victims. "Fayden," I uttered, exposing myself in clear view.

The Hmong quickly fixed eyes and muzzle on me, then lowered his weapon. Moving closer, it was apparent that Fayden had beat us to the punch. He'd ambushed the Pathet-Lao at what appeared to be point-blank range. One man's head was shredded like a red cabbage.

I turned, hearing a rustle in the thicket, and saw Lok and Pug. I gave them a quick arm signal indicating for them to move back up the trail and monitor the approach.

Turning my attention to Fayden, I saw him rise slowly and take aim on the supine figure he'd been talking to.

"Ho, Fayden," I blurted, seeing that the man was still alive. I moved forward and knelt beside him. His gut was soaked with a glistening pool of dark blood. His lips quivered like he was trying to beg but the words wouldn't come out.

I glanced around the sprawled carnage looking for a Havelock cap. It appeared all the patrol members were wearing folded, black scarfs, but it was impossible to tell what cabbage head had been wearing.

I yanked a pen from my shirt pocket, quickly sketched a block-style cap on my palm, then drew in the neck covering at the rear of the cap.

"Okay, you scum-sucking pig," I uttered through gritted teeth while fixing my gaze on the wide-eyed man and holding my palm out in front of him. "I want the son-of-a-bitch who wears this!"

I knew the communist probably couldn't understand English but the eyes told me he got the picture. The man's tongue lapped at his lips as he blinked, darting terrified glances back and forth from my palm to the AK muzzle Fayden had pointed at him.

"Where?" I blurted. "Where?"

Bubbles and bloody snot streamed out his nose. "Nee—nee lat lon . . . Na . . . Dao. Lat lon Na Dao," he groaned.

I frowned. "Na Dao? Na Dao?"

The man moved his head lethargically, nodding yes. I stood and looked at Fayden—his finger was poised on the trigger. Angry furrows of skin gripped his wet brow. The kill was rightfully his. I nodded and moved away to search the other bodies.

A second later a single shot cracked through the dismal haze and I breathed the faint scent of gunsmoke; the scent of a father's revenge.

Searching the bodies, I found some Laotian currency along with a bloodstained, hand-drawn map of the area.

Using Lok and Pug to assist us, we carried the bodies off the trail and hid them in dense thicket near a stream. My underlying hope was that the bodies would lure any

predators away from us as well as prevent any follow-up
Pathet-Lao patrols from discovering the ambush.

As Fayden and I struggled to carry the last body into
the dense undergrowth, I decided to supplement our
Pathet-Lao impersonation with an additional costume.
Placing the last body near the others, I glanced at Lok.
"How about taking the clothes off that one," I said, pointing to the corpse that appeared to have the least blood-
soaked garments.

Turning, I looked at Rham. "Go back and make sure
that trail is clean. Bring the AKs here."

I pulled a fresh magazine from one of the KIA's vests
and handed it to Fayden. "You better reload," I said,
tapping his AK magazine.

*"Du-me,"* Lok exclaimed with an amused voice as he
jerked the pants off the corpse. "Dis VC bitch."

I stepped closer, looking down at the sparse trace of
hair between her legs. "No doubt about that," I muttered.

Lok grabbed her head, pulling her torso forward while
I knelt and helped him take the bloodstained shirt off.
"Wash these in that stream over there," I said, releasing
the naked torso and letting it drop back into the leaves.

I stood and saw Rham carrying the four enemy AK-47s.
I took one of them, quickly removed the receiver guide
cover, then pushed the recoil spring guide assembly forward and released the tension. I pulled the long assembly
out and heaved it into the foliage.

Within seconds, Rham and I had disabled all four AKs.
Lok hurried forward and handed me the enemy garments.

Stuffing the small wad of wet clothes into my side pants
pocket, I asked, "Rham, is that trail clean?"

"Tail clee."

I reached and picked up a magazine vest, handed it to
Fayden, then glanced around. "Okay, let's hook 'em out
of here, gang. Rham, take point and keep us off the trail,
amigo."

# Chapter 14

After linking up with the team, we moved quietly through the cool rain and paralleled the river until we located what appeared to be a good place to cross. I moved the team back a distance from the trail, then sent Pug, Ski, and Lok to make the river recon. I told Ski to provide security as Pug and Lok crossed.

After they left, I pulled the small, enemy map from my pocket. The blood stains made it difficult to analyze. It was sketched with lines, dots, X's and several symbols that resembled the letter "Y." There was no evidence of topography except for a couple of larger, abstract contours which I took to represent the rough outline of mountains.

I passed the map to Tuong. "See if you can make heads or tails out of this. I'm going back to check on Ski," I said, standing.

Taking a step away, my curiosity nudged me. I turned and looked down at Tuong. When I had found Fayden at his ambush site on the trail he was squatted talking to one of the wounded Pats. "Try to find out what that was about if you can."

Tuong nodded, then leaned toward Fayden, showing him the map and talking softly while moving his finger over the paper.

I walked on looking for Binkowski. I found him taking

a piss by the river. Beyond him Lok and Pug were wading, waist deep, back across the forty-foot, jade-colored expanse of water. Easing down the muddy bank, I saw Ski pick up his rifle and turn to check Pug and Lok's progress.

"Mister clean," I whispered.

He glanced back at me. "Window screen."

"Did base have anything for us during that last contact?" I asked, moving to his side.

"Roger. But it's like they just keep telling us what we already know," he answered. "I mean, you already told me that guy Ho or whatever his name—"

"Ha," I interjected softly.

"Yeah, Ha. Well, you said that Ha said that an Okie team was working north of here and that's what base had for us." He paused, reading my eyes, then added, "Nothing about Duell."

I turned my attention to watch as Pug and Lok neared mid-stream. The rush of current against their bodies looked to be about five knots.

"By the way, why are we going to cross this river?" Ski whispered while adjusting his rifle sling over his neck.

Squinting, I scanned the opposite bank. "According to Fayden, this river flows on past Na Dao. We're going to ease our way down there and see if we can't grab us a prisoner."

"A prisoner? But—but this isn't a snatch mission. Why are we . . . oh, I get it. Once we get him we're going to interrogate him and try to find out if he knows anything about Abraham Duell. Right?"

Ski's estimation of my intent was only partially correct, but there was no need to tip my hand about it now. "That's right. But it may not be a him. It could be a her. It's difficult to tell the difference until you take off their pants," I answered.

"You mean they got gir, girls working with them too?" Ski responded, looking down as if to see if he'd buttoned his fly.

"That's affirm, partner. There was one with that patrol that Fayden nailed."

"And—and you took her pants off? Why did you take her—"

"We may need to fine tune our disguise later. The clothes may come in handy."

"How did she look?" Ski asked, grinning.

"Like any other skinny, little, communist bitch."

"Gosh," he muttered. "Wish I'd been there. You know how I like Oriental girls. I mean don't—don't get me wrong, Brett. I'm not into nec, necterphobia . . ."

"Necrophilia?" I supplied, grabbing a branch and leaning to reach a hand outward to Lok as he neared the riverbank.

"Yeah. I'm not into that."

"How's it look over there?" I asked, pulling Lok up onto the bank while Ski assisted Rham.

Lok grinned. "Look good, Sar Brett. No see tak."

I'd instructed Lok and Rham to check the opposite side closely for Pathet-Lao and tiger tracks. I estimated that the steep incline on the other side of the river made it an undesirable zone of travel. Also, we'd be less likely to be observed moving down through that area—Fayden had confirmed earlier that the terrain east of the river had no trails.

Leaving Ski, Pug, and Lok at the river to maintain security, I headed back to bring the remainder of the team to the crossing.

Tuong stood as I approached. "Fayden say him no understan what say here, Sar Brett," he said, holding the map before me while continuing. "But I'm tink maybe dis be pla where Pat-Lao stay slee." He pointed to the various X's on the paper.

"That's possible. How about these?" I asked, pointing to the marks that resembled a "Y".

"I'm tink dis where Pat-Lao knowing Hmong bring yaying."

"You mean like an assembly area where they bring the opium to sell?"

"Rogee. But I'm not know why Pat-Lao wan know and make mark for opey."

I folded the paper and shoved it into my pocket. "I don't know either, but you did good, babysan."

He grinned. "Yes. Liking you say, I x-cep-in-al sometime."

"Okay, exceptional. Did you find out what he was talking to that wounded Pat-Lao about?"

Tuong turned his back to Fayden. "Yes. Him say one time he work for dat Lao man when buil road here call hi-wa sex. And him say to man dat sum Pat-Lao kill all and kill him son and wibe and dat why him now kill all Pat-Lao."

I'd known that the French and Laotians had used Hmong labor to do road construction in years past. It seemed poetic justice that Fayden would end up killing his former road boss turned Pathet-Lao.

"Well, the bastard should have stuck with the highway department instead of taking up with the communists. He got what was coming to him. Let's *dee*," I said, reaching to heave my rucksack up onto my shoulder.

I sent Tuong and Fayden on to the river while I went to recover Phan from his trail vigil position.

Peering through the wet shadows, I saw Phan squatted, faithfully studying the dim approach. "Puck you," I whispered, using the individualized challenge for Phan.

"Puck you too," he responded, standing. "Look see I'm find here," he said while showing me an expended 7.62 round.

I examined the brass. Taking into consideration the ones Tuong had found, it was now my ballpark guess that the local Pats were probably having trouble with tigers also. I tossed the cartridge away. "Let's go take a bath, babysan."

"Take bat? Why we take bat?"

"Because it's the only way to cross the river, partner."

When we got to the team, I sent Lok and Pug across first to secure the other side. I decided to send two personnel across at a time in order to provide max security during crossing.

As soon as Lok gave me the all-clear signal for the other side, I motioned Tuong and Fayden down to the water's edge. Seeing my signal to enter the river, Fayden ran back up the bank nodding his head and waving his rifle.

I frowned, not understanding the obvious display of emotion. "Tuong, what's his problem?" I asked, looking around to inspect the water for any signs of danger. "Look, if he can't swim, tell him it's no big deal. We're walking across. It's okay."

Tuong walked up the bank to talk with Fayden. I followed.

After a moment Tuong turned. "Sar Brett, him no wan go in water."

"No shit, I've guessed that much already. Ask him what the problem is."

"I'm know deez people, Sar Brett. Dae tink if go in water good speer-ee wash away from body and dae maybe die soon."

I shoved my bush hat back on my head feeling my whole parade coming to a halt. "You're saying that he thinks that if he goes in the river his good—his protective—spirits will be washed off? Is that right?"

"Rogee, Sar Brett," Tuong answered timidly.

"Well, well," I muttered. "What does he think this rain has been doing to his protective coating? Shit, it washes things off too!"

"I understand it, Brett," Binkowski chimed in.

"Of course you do, Arnold. It's fucking superstition! How about calling your grandmother and ask what she'd do about this."

"Well, maybe we could build a bridge. That would work," he chimed again.

I scowled at Ski. "Dammit, Arnold, I don't have an engineer company with me.

"Tuong, ask him if there is a bridge anywhere around here."

Fayden's response was cheerful, but the news wasn't—the closest bridge was near the village of Na Dao.

"I know," Ski said, stepping forward. "I'll carry him across."

I turned, looking at Ski. "You may just have accidentally restored my faith in you, partner.

"Tuong, ask Fayden if he minds being carried across. No, no wait . . . don't say it that way. Tell him the Gods say he'll be fine if Ski carries him across. Tell him the Gods trust Ski."

After Tuong spoke, Fayden pondered plan B while scrutinizing Binkowski like a Russian inspecting a new tractor. I knew Ski could handle it—his flat back bench press was 380 pounds and he did strict squats with 500.

Finally, Fayden reluctantly agreed to the arrangement. Ski gave me his rucksack and the two LAWs, and passed the three CAR-15s he was carrying to Tuong. He then knelt down to help the Hmong onto his back.

As he entered the water with Fayden, Ski's foot slipped slightly on the muddy bank.

"Careful, Ski," I coached, stepping in behind him. "The spirits and I are counting on you, buddy."

# Chapter 15

By 0915 hours we had tripped, stumbled, and clawed our way over the steep, thickly-foliaged area leading south along the river. We hadn't seen any tracks—man or beast—which didn't surprise me because the terrain was more suited to eagles.

I called a chow break and moved the team into a tight circle beneath a large teak tree. As we mixed our LRPRs, I decided it was time to level with the team about my intentions and at the same time let Fayden know that I needed him to play a pivotal role in my plan. The incident at the river crossing had convinced me to be careful about taking my conjectures for reality when dealing with the Hmong. If, for some reason, Fayden couldn't, or wouldn't, be a part of the plan, I needed to know about it now, before another wad of defecation hit the cooling apparatus.

Before eating, I had Binkowski and Rham make a quick, circular recon of our position. When they came back, Rham gave me a thumbs up indicating the area was clear.

Ski sat down near me whispering emphatically, "Brett, you wouldn't believe the size of the snake I just saw out there! I mean that thing was as thick as one of those LAWs and musta been twenty feet long. It looked like it could have been a python."

"Probably was," I replied, pouring water into my LRPR bag and stirring it.

"You mean they got pythons out here too? Don't they swim, I mean, like water?"

"Roger that."

"Well, in that case I'm not too keen on going back in that river again."

"Try not to loose any hair about it, partner. This is only your second trip into Laos. Consider it part of your field zoo training."

"You no worry, Skee. You too ugly for to eat," Phan added.

"That's great, Phan. I feel better already," Ski said. "By the way, why are we carrying these LAWs and those extra Claymores, Brett?"

I knew eventually Ski would want to know about the extra arms. His question came at a time when I'd be able to give him a complete answer without any bullshit about it.

"Let's eat. I'll explain it in a minute, partner, but the main reason we're carrying the extra gear is because we're going to use it," I said, glancing around at my team as I ate. Tuong was sharing his ration with Fayden. It seemed, despite the mild communications gap we had with Fayden, that the team accepted him as one of us, and that he felt the same. Now my team needed to know that I was about to put them squarely into what amounted to "unwarranted jeopardy." This mission was supposed to have been a kind of cakewalk compared to what we normally did—it was supposed to have been an easy five-day stroll in the woods, avoiding enemy contact and looking for Abraham Duell. But things had changed. A village of innocent people, whose only crime was trying to scratch a meager existence out of the soil, had been ruthlessly slaughtered, and I took that about as personally as a razor blade slicing across my forehead.

As everyone finished their meal, I folded my ration bag and slid it into the side pouch of my ruck.

"Listen up, gang," I said, letting my gaze drift to each face as I spoke. "You're all aware that yesterday, this man's village, his family, his friends, his everything was wiped out by the Pat-Lao." I paused, looking up at the canopy of branches above me, then lowered my head to look first at Fayden, then the others. "I can't feel what this man is feeling, but I know it must be about the toughest feeling anyone has to endure.

"It pisses me off full-bore that anybody can do that, massacre a village, and get away with it, and, the fact is, gents, they are not going to get away with it!" I glanced at Ski. "The reason we took on this extra gear is because I plan to raid and kill every Pat-Lao I can, right where they are now making their local headquarters, in Na Dao."

"Wait a minute," Binkowski broke in. "If—if we do that, won't we kill innocent villagers down there? And that's like—"

"Just listen, Ski. No, it will not, because with Fayden's help I plan on evacuating the village before I hit.

"Also, if you'll notice, I am not using the word *we*. No one on this team is being asked or expected to be a part of this." I moved my finger around the circle. "You, and me too for that matter, are paid to perform the duties and missions that SOG tells us to do. Understand, this is *not* a SOG mission. This is my decision, my mission.

"Yesterday I was hot and half-cocked to kick ass and kill anything that got in my way. Today I'm a shade cooler, because I realize that is what it's going to take in order to pull this off—cool precision.

"Now that I've said all that, I'll say this. Any man who wants to stay with me is welcome. Otherwise I'm going to request exfiltration for you tomorrow morning."

"But—but . . . we can't exfil without you!" Ski exclaimed.

"Sure you can. You simply get on the chopper, tell them

I'm MIA, and go home. I'll eventually link up with either RT Anaconda, Vang Pao, or the Agency and get back. No sweat.''

"Well, shit! That's great!" Ski said standing abruptly. "You've got it all thought out, don't you? But what about Duell? You know that's our mission, you know! And—''

"Sar Brett, I'm can say sum-ting?" Rham asked, ignoring Binkowski's outburst.

"Shoot," I answered, nodding at him.

"I'm understan what you say. I'm knowing you signee x-tende paper stay Vietnam wid us. Now, I'm stay wid you.''

Without hesitation, Phan, Lok, and Tuong followed suit. They looked up at Binkowski who was standing with his mouth half open staring down toward the river.

Looking back at us, he gave us all his famous, lopsided grin. "What the heck," he said, shrugging. "I'm part of this team. I mean, besides, you can't call an exfil for just me. Count me in.''

"You good man, Skee. You make ryh sission," Lok quipped.

I was glad we'd maintained team integrity. I briefly answered Ski's earlier question about Duell, telling him that although I hadn't completely written Duell off, it was my gut feeling that Duell was probably dead or a guest at the Hanoi Hilton. I finished by saying, "We're here, so we might as well give these local, communist bastards a refresher course in Special Forces tactical gymnastics and firepower. *Sat-cong*!''

"*Sat-cong!*" the Cowboys chorused, slapping the barrel guards of their AKs.

"*Sat-cong,*" Ski repeated. "I'm not real sure what it means but—''

" 'Death to communists' is what that means," I said, shifting a glance to Fayden, then Tuong. "Babysan, what I need to know now is if Fayden is with us. Ask him if he will help us kill communists and make sure he understands that we need his help all the way through this.

"And while you're at it, tell him what *sat-cong* means. He's already got four notches to his credit. He might as well know we're all on the same sheet of music."

As Tuong conveyed my message to Fayden, I watched the Hmong's eyes. There was little doubt in my mind that he would help us; my concern was making sure that he would maintain a disciplined adherence to my plan and not get trigger-happy every time he saw the enemy. His ambush had already proven that he could act with quick and deadly accuracy when confronting the enemy, but could he control his wrath long enough to follow orders and help set the stage for a mass extermination of Pathet-Lao?

Before moving onward, I had loosely determined that Fayden was with us and that he understood the need to follow orders. With that solace, I'd decided to put the Hmong on point with Tuong with instructions to take us to a good area of observation overlooking the village of Na Dao. I hadn't briefed the team on my concept of the operation yet; I'd decided to wait and assemble as much intel on the target area and enemy concentration before laying out our actions at the objective. The mission briefing at NKP had slotted us for a maximum of six days in the AO and the clock was now running on day five. We needed to act fast.

I knew I could stretch our allotted time on target by sending a false message informing SOG that I was in pursuit of "pertinent intelligence" related to Duell. But that stretch factor potential would be blown out of the saddle if Duell was suddenly found; SOG would subsequently transmit an exfiltration order to us.

Considering that the enemy was now aware of our presence, it wouldn't be long before they heated up a plan for hot pursuit. Time was of the essence and the sooner we hit, the better.

"Tuong, tell Fayden that the first thing we need is a prisoner. Also, I need to know approximately how many Hmong are in that village. Ask him if we're going to have a problem getting them to move out.

"By the way," I added, reaching into my pocket and withdrawing the wet, enemy garments. "Here's a little something to help spruce up your costume. When we go in to make the snatch, I want you decked out in these."

"Rogee," Tuong replied, unfolding the wadded clothes.

As Tuong went through a discussion with Fayden, I took my map out and updated it with our newfound river. "Ski, get your map. I'll draw in that trail and the river," I said, folding mine.

Moving closer, Binkowski handed me the map. "Brett, have you got a plan worked out yet or is this a play-it-by-ear routine?"

"Partner, this is too critical to try and tap dance through," I answered, looking at Phan, signaling for him to take Rham and make another perimeter check. As they crept out, I moved closer to Ski, showing him our location. At the same time, I briefed Ski on my intended prep phase. I told him phase one, which I intended to enact this morning, would have two purposes—one: to view and recon the western edge of Na Dao village; two: to try and snatch a prisoner.

Ski nodded as I spoke; he seemed to take on a more alert focus to the situation. I told him that when I got a better target assessment and hopefully reliable information from a prisoner, I'd develop phase two, and after that I'd plan our actions at the objective.

When I finished, Ski tossed another question disguised as a suggestion. "Brett, shouldn't we . . . I mean I know it sounds like I'm still harping on the original mission but—but shouldn't we try to make sure that Duell isn't in there, the village I mean, before we hit it?"

"Roger that. It's my feeling that between the interrogation and Tuong and Fayden's personal inspection of the village, that we'll be able to determ.ne if Duell is being held there.''

"And if he is . . . then what?''

"Then we slip in, pull him out, and start the fireworks. But, like I said before, partner, I th.nk Abe Duell is as gone as a wild goose in winter. At any rate, the Pats are going to know the pros from Dover were definitely in town.''

I thought back to the prudent words that our commander, Colonel Ivan Kahn, always whipped on us before we boarded a chopper for insertion: "Remember, it always takes longer than you expect, it always costs more than you anticipate, and just to be safe, don't forget to take a good, healthy piss afterward.''

I reminded myself that most rural tribes in Southeast Asia did not have a good sense of time or timing—for that reason I would have to keep one of the Cowboys, preferably Tuong, with Fayden during critical phases of the operation.

Tuong finished his talk with Fayden and moved to a squatting position beside me. "Sar Brett, him say maybe sex-tee pe-po in village and say dae no like Pat-Lao but can do noting when Pat-Lao come. Him say maybe no problem to get pe-po to go away from village—if dae know we kill Pat-Lao.''

Tuong's assessment about "no problem'' omitted what I knew could very well turn into a problem. The villagers' exit had to be quite expeditious, but it would be difficult to prevent them from taking all their personal belongings with them if they knew I planned to blow the place into the next grid square.

I didn't plan on lying about the scenar.o. However, telling the whole truth was not feasible. I figured that the Na Dao villagers could be relocated to Fayden's village, temporarily at least, so I wasn't putting them out on the street.

"Okay, Tuong. Tonight you and Fayden will go into Na Dao and explain our intentions to the elders. Let them know that they can return to their village in one day. You'll have to make sure they understand that they must leave the village quietly; no bags and baggage, okay?''

"But, Brett," Ski butted in. "Won't that village be imposs—''

"Silence is golden, Arnold! Just listen. Their exit needs to begin at 0200 hours.''

Tuong frowned. "What we do abou guards?''

"You and Fayden will knife-kill them. I'll explain more after we've made our target recon. Y'all get ready to move out.''

With Fayden on point, followed by Tuong, we carefully traversed the steep, windswept terrain another two klicks. Rounding a section of the mountain, we found a well-concealed spot above the river and about 300 meters northwest of the area where we'd RON'd the first night.

After putting out a four-corner security on our position, I sat huddled with Tuong and Fayden, studying Na Dao with my binoculars. I quickly realized why I hadn't seen the river during our previous observation. Part of the tributary ran underground nearing the village, and the exposed section was partially obscured by tall trees.

The rain had given us a break during our movement, but dark clouds still continued to dominate the sky, threatening another downpour. Scanning the area, I saw a rag-tag group of Pats march route-step out of the village toward the grassy area which served as an airfield. I studied their heads—Harry was AWOL. The dozen or so troops stopped at the far end of the field and began setting up what appeared to be homemade target silhouettes. Moments later, they assembled and sat down facing the targets. A stout man then took a standing position in front of the group. "Looks like some of the Bowery Boys are about to get a little open air classroom time,'' I whispered.

"What they do?" Tuong queried.

"Well, they've all got AKs. I'd guess it's range firing time."

The appearance of a firing lesson indicated that the Pats were not low on ammo, but the absence of B-40 rockets was a positive indication that perhaps they were in short supply. Commonly, the Pat-Lao followed the same organizational structure as the NVA, and that meant a B-40 rocket team was integral to patrols. Neither of the two patrols we'd already observed had been equipped with rockets—I wasn't about to get too optimistic, but I hoped it stayed that way. Months ago I'd been on the receiving end of a B-40. The awesome projectile hit a teak tree that I was taking cover behind and instantly turned it into a mass of toothpicks.

Moving my field glasses back over the village, I examined the Hmong. The ones I could see reminded me of the former inhabitants of Chung's village—old men, women, and children. A large group of soldiers was gathered around a table outside a hut near the northern edge of the hamlet. Another class I guessed.

"What do you see? Anything?" Ski asked quietly, moving the brush toward us.

Keeping the binoculars focused on the gathering, I replied, "Roger. Plenty of Pats. The good news is I haven't seen a pith helmet or a B-40 . . . yet."

I handed the field glasses to Tuong. "Check it out, and ask Fayden where that bridge is he was telling us about. I didn't see it anywhere down there."

The distant, sporadic crackle of single-shot, AK fire brought my attention back to the range class. They were now strung along the firing line about seventy meters from the targets.

"What's that, a . . . damn, Brett . . . it—it looks like they're executing some people down there," Ski muttered excitedly.

"Negative, partner. It's just a range firing class."

"Oh," Ski said, squinting for a better look.

"Sar Brett, Fayden say breegee that way, little way."
Tuong's arm motioned to the area beyond the trees that
hid a section of the river. "No can see from dis place."

"How far is little way?"

"Maybe five-minute walk from village."

"Okay, see that sloped area on the north side?"

"Rogee."

"You see it, Ski?"

"Roger."

"We're going to move down there and try to get into
that tall grass. Babysan, give Ski those binoculars. You
need to change into your new costume. It's time to see if
we can't find us a prisoner to interview."

# Chapter 16

We learned from Fayden that the open field areas located east and west of the village were used to cultivate opium and that the fall crop had just been planted. He told us that a westerly-oriented foot path skirted the field and turned southwest toward a wooded area at the sloped base of a mountain. The wooded area had been partially cleared of large trees in preparation for another field to be used for spring cultivation. The tree clearing project had been suspended some months ago when the able-bodied men had to flee to escape the Pat-Lao recruiters. According to Fayden, it was this zone that the Pats commonly traveled when initiating patrols southward into the mountains.

In addition to the normal assortment of pigs, chickens, and dogs, I'd counted roughly sixty armed communists in the village—it was impossible to guess how many more personnel were out on patrol. I decided to move the team into the partially cleared area and try snagging a prisoner.

As we moved down through the southwestern tree line, I wondered how long it would take before the Pats started missing the patrol which Fayden had nailed. If their patrol duration was one day, then by tonight the Pats would be absent four faces at the dinner table and that would alert them. I couldn't second-guess what their reaction would be, but knowing the Pathet-Lao, I doubted that they would mount an all-out search unless cousin Chuck showed up to motivate them.

Pondering the tactical situation, I surmised that the advantages we had were the element of surprise and the absence of NVA. The communists knew that SOG had never directed a personnel assault on concentrated enemy positions in Laos. They also knew that SOG never implemented arc lights in the area of Hmong villages without prior coordination with friendly forces. If our allies in Laos approved an arc light target, their forces would relocate the inhabitants long before the 750- and 500-pound bombs started tearing up the landscape.

In essence, the Pathet-Lao were clever. They had hidden among the Hmong at Na Dao and become untouchable—that status was about to get crushed like a safe dropping out of a seventh story window.

The damp, morning air laced with the fumes of village cooking fires clung to my breath as we moved over the muddy terrain. An invisible chorus of birds squawked and chirped from lofty morning shadows like anxious spectators awaiting a foray.

After moving out of the tree line, we passed through elephant grass and found the path. In accordance with our SOP, Rham, who was sharing point with Fayden, halted the team beside the trail. I moved forward to examine the danger area before crossing.

"See no tak," Rham whispered as I knelt at his side.

I leaned out from the cloak of wet grass, peering left then right. The trail was a mesh of mud and grass about eighteen inches wide which ribboned through the five-foot-high grass bordering the field.

Motioning Tuong forward, I spoke softly. "You and Fayden go down the trail and get into a good watch spot. When you see someone coming this way, get down here fast and let me know if it's Pat-Lao or a villager."

He grinned. "Rogee, Sar Brett. How long you wan we stay?"

I checked my watch: 1105 hours. "I'll send Lok down to you in one hour if we haven't had any movement through here. We'll be on the other side of this trail."

I then made a subtle movement of my eyes toward Fayden. "Watch him, babysan," I said softly. "Don't let him get trigger happy. Know what I mean?"

"I'm understan. Him be okay I'm tink."

I winked and tapped Tuong's shoulder. "Your new outfit looks good, but you keep your ass out of sight for now. Go."

After crossing the trail, I positioned Binkowski and Phan thirty meters farther down as an additional LP for anyone who might approach from that direction. My reasoning in crossing the path took into consideration the possibility that someone could discover our tracks and follow us into the elephant grass. Now, if they were to pursue us, at least we'd see them before they got here.

Rham provided rear security while Lok and I nestled into a prone position a few feet off the path and waited.

Forty minutes later, strong winds gusted through the field. The breezes lashed at the grass, blowing water residue off the tall, green blades and spraying our faces. I lowered my head, pulling the bush hat downward over my brow to avoid the windy sting. Thunder signaled more rain was about to move in.

Tuong's hurried whisper cut through the wind as he scurried into my position. "We seeing two Pat-Lao, Sar Brett."

"Where?"

"Dae go in ground."

"You mean a tunnel?"

"No . . . liking in bunker where Hmong keep sum tool for working."

I turned my attention to Lok while yanking my rucksack off. "Get Rham up here with you, then tell Ski I'm moving in to make a snatch. Y'all hang tight 'til I get back."

Jumping to a crouched stance, I moved out onto the path and followed Tuong's rapid pace. As we approached Fayden, he arm-signaled us to follow him. Clatters of thunder briefly concealed the rustling noise of our hurried movement into the knee-high grass. Seconds later the rain began.

Nearing the edge of the grass line, Fayden halted and dropped to one knee. He frowned, slapped his AK stock, then jabbed with a clenched fist toward a mound in the center of the large, triangular-shaped field. He then made a downward motion with his hand.

I guessed his hand gesture was telling me that the Pats had gone into what appeared to be the Hmong version of a storm cellar. I didn't understand why he'd slapped his AK, but for a moment it seemed he was implying that he intended to shoot the Pats.

I held two fingers up, then motioned toward the mound. Fayden nodded.

Leaning toward Tuong, I said, "Before we move in, you make sure he understands we need to take a prisoner. No firing unless we have to."

Tuong took a step toward Fayden and gently lowered the muzzle of his rifle. He quietly relayed my message. I felt it was best to re-emphasize our intentions rather than risk the possibility of Fayden drifting off frequency and killing our potential prisoner.

Peering into the gray shroud of rain, it occurred to me that my apprehension about Fayden's sense of control and discipline was probably wrong. It was more likely me trying to conceal the self-doubt churning inside my gut. Ugly memories of Chung, his mother, and the dead children twisted through my mind like a rusty corkscrew. I knew that when I came face to face with the scum out there that I'd have to fight myself from the gripping urge to drive my blue-bladed steel up their gullets and into their fetid brains. A covert-killing-techniques instructor once told me: "There is no instrument of death more beautifully personal than a knife."

Tuong turned, speaking softly. "Sar Brett. Him understan, no kill."

I nodded. "Good. Now, where is the entrance to the storage shed?"

He blinked at me. "What mean sto—"

"The bunker where they keep the tools . . . where's the door?"

Tuong's gaze followed mine into the field. "Door on other end, Fayden say."

"Okay. Listen up. I'm going to move over there and look-see. I want you and Fayden to stay right here 'til I signal you to come.

"When you get to my position, tell Fayden to get down and keep watch. You and I will burst in and give 'em a good vertical butt stroke across the head." I jerked the butt of my rifle slightly upward toward Tuong's head to demonstrate how I wanted it done. He grinned.

"If I get in the shit out there, you cover me."

"Rogee."

I stepped out of the grass into the ankle-deep mud and moved swiftly through the dense rain toward the mound. Approaching the bunker shed, I could see thatched layers of grass covering the structure. Dropping to my knees at the rear of the low roof, I quickly scanned the misty field looking for any signs of movement. None. Only the rain-pelted sway of tall grass stirred through the gray haze.

I stood and edged closer to the entrance. I tensed, glancing down at my selector switch. I gently pushed the selector from auto to semi—if the Pats suddenly emerged from the shelter and I had to fire, I couldn't risk a loud, full-auto burst.

Nearing the entrance, I saw that the door was nothing more than a large piece of canvas. Muffled voices and groans filtered from behind the door curtain. I raised from my crouched stance and waved a signal toward the grass line.

Tuong and Fayden darted swiftly from the cloak of grass through the misty haze toward me. Fayden knelt at the end of the shelter. Tuong flipped me a thumbs-up as his catlike steps crept closer. With a slow movement of my head, I motioned for him to follow me while I took a cautious step to the front of the doorway. My eyes quickly scanned the rain-veiled distance looking for any approaching figures. I nodded a ready signal at Tuong, then eased my rifle muzzle to the side of the door flap.

Jerking the canvas away, I lunged down into the dim grotto, getting a whiff of stale, opium smoke and immediately seeing the quick motion of naked buttocks thrusting between two bare, vertical legs.

"Having a nooner, asshole?" I jeered, ramming my boot into his butt like a drop-kicked football.

The jolting force of my kick sent his wiry body rolling sideways, revealing the naked girl. She froze, gaping at my rifle muzzle with quivering lips.

Thruster leaped for his AK, promptly intersecting my boot as I round-house kicked him across the face.

"Aheee!" he cried, clutching his nose and slumping backward against a pile of burlap sacks. His wilting erection looked like the pride of the Leprechauns.

"Not your day is it, pixie?" I said, reaching to grab the AK and toss it out of his reach.

Looking around, I saw the wide-eyed girl staring down at the rifle barrel Tuong held pressed against her stomach.

He grinned. "They try do boom-boom, Sar Brett," he smirked down at the girl. "You like boom-boom? I giving you boom-boom here," he said, prodding the AK muzzle lower to her pubic region.

"In America we call this catching them with their pants down," I muttered while moving to the doorway. I opened the flap and stepped outside to feel cool rain spatter my face. Alongside the shelter I saw Fayden still kneeling at his vigil point.

Ducking back inside, I glared at the bloody-faced male. "Tuong, tell the anuses to get their clothes on. They're coming with us."

# Chapter 17

With our prisoners in tow, we trekked out into the pelting monsoon, rejoined the team, and moved to a high area about seventy meters above our previous observation spot.

Casanova Little-Dick had sustained a broken nose and was very cooperative during our movement; the girl wasn't. Prior to our exit from the shelter she had emphatically told Tuong that she was not Pathet-Lao. Her young features, clothes, and dialect confirmed that she was Hmong, but I wasn't taking any chances. When I'd broken in on their horizontal bop she was crooning like a hoot owl.

We'd gagged them, tied their hands, and put a slip-knot leash around their necks. The male was the only one with a weapon. A search of his clothing produced a faded *chieuhoi* pass, some kip, and a small pocket knife. In his haste to get to the low-rent rendezvous, he'd either forgotten his magazine vest or didn't consider it important.

Fayden located a rock overhang at the base of a limestone cliff to shelter us from the rain during interrogation. I separated the prisoners immediately, sending the girl away with Ski and Lok while Tuong, Fayden, and I concentrated on the male.

As Ski started to lead the girl away, I noticed his anxious focus on the swollen nipples protruding from her thin, wet shirt. "Arnold," I said, snapping him from his near-drooling trance. "I know she's a little fox and I know how you like Oriental girls, but keep your mind on the mission. Roger?"

Ski gave me a smirking grin as if he remembered our last trip into North Vietnam. "Roger, Brett, got it. Mind on the mission."

I nodded. During the last mission we'd linked up with a beautiful CAS agent who wanted to give us a little more than "pertinent intelligence" about the target—when I'd left Ski alone with her one afternoon he'd accepted her favors.

I told Ski to take up a position near the rounded base of the cliff and maintain max security. I informed him that we'd come get the girl when we finished with the male. My intention was to question them both separately and see if their answers correlated.

Turning my attention back to Casanova, I knelt and removed his gag, then applied a field dressing to his bloody nose. I really didn't give a flying fuck if the bastard bled to death or not, but I'd learned in a class on Methods of Interrogation that it was sometimes beneficial to show concern for the prisoner in order to gain information.

Finished with my quick-patch medical handiwork, I glanced at Tuong who was squatted beside Fayden peering at the Pat. "Babysan, ask this turkey what his name is."

The prisoner's answer was lengthy and emphatic, complete with smiles and polite glances at me. I guessed he was telling more than just his name. Several times he raised his bound hands and made a contorted version of a praying gesture to me.

"Sar Brett, him say name, Sap."

I almost laughed. "Sap. Great name, fits him perfectly. What else did Sap have to say?"

"Him say him not Pat-Lao. Him have to work for dem or maybe dae kill him."

Sap kept his best pleading look directed at me while

Tuong spoke. He avoided looking at Fayden who had a frown directed at him that could break glass.

I took a canteen from my web gear, opened it, and passed it to Sap. "That seems to be the same general story that his girlfriend told us, babysan."

"I'm tink him full a bull-shee, Sar Brett."

"Me too, partner. But for now, let's let him think we believe him. Ask him how many Pat-Lao are in the village and why they're there."

A dozen questions later, Sap had laid out his version of the local Pathet-Lao purpose for securing Na Dao. He informed us that they were awaiting an NVA truck which was bringing a "big gun" to shoot down airplanes. He said that there were seventy soldiers in Na Dao with the mission to secure the area and begin digging a large hole to be used as a crater encasement for what I guessed was going to be a 37mm anti-aircraft position.

The story sounded reasonable. During the past year there had been a significant increase in anti-aircraft gun placements, both 23- and 37mm. As a result, our aircraft losses had jumped by twenty percent.

There was no doubt that the gun Sap described was a 37—I'd seen one up close on my first mission across the fence. It was a towed, four-wheel, artillery piece which usually required a three-man crew. The four-wheel configuration of the weapon gave it greater stability under firing conditions than its little brother version, the two-wheeled 23mm gun. The most awesome characteristic of the 37 was that it fired what were called "second-chance" rounds—the projectiles could be pre-set to explode at varied altitudes which meant that if it didn't make a direct hit, there was still a chance of aerial-exploded shrapnel damaging the targeted aircraft.

"Find out when this big gun is supposed to be here," I said, keeping my tone casual while taking a pen from my pocket.

Tuong talked quietly with Sap while I wiped the dirt off

my hand, then sketched a second rendition of a Havelock cap on my palm.

"Him say two day ago sa-pose to be here. Him tink *beaucoup* rain make prob-lum to come."

"So the rain has made them late. That's reasonable," I said, tucking the pen away. I stared at Sap before revealing my palm artwork. So far everything he'd told us made sense, except his denial of being a communist, and even that was a justifiable fabrication considering he was staring at three loaded rifles.

I noticed Fayden slowly stroking the wet muzzle of his AK as if he was ready to put a burst into Sap. Up until now he'd been patient, but I could tell it was wearing thin.

I thought back to the moment on the trail when I'd questioned the wounded Pat about Havelock Harry; my question was worded to imply that there was only one specific man who wore that style cap. It now occurred to me that I'd been taking my conjecture for reality—although I didn't like admitting it, I realized that it was possible that more than one man wore a Havelock.

I showed my palm to Tuong, then to Sap. "Ask him how many Pat-Lao wear a hat like this, babysan."

A second later I had my answer: one. Sap informed us that the man's name was Tinbac and that Tinbac was a patrol leader. He also said that Tinbac was not liked by the others and that he always tried to avoid being assigned patrol duty with him.

Keeping a poker face leveled at Sap, I spoke softly. "Ask our boy Sap when was the last time he was on patrol with Tinbac."

I watched Sap's eyes closely as Tuong relayed the question. I thought back, trying to remember the faces I'd seen in the shadows when Tinbac's patrol had passed—blank. If Sap answered yesterday, then our interview was over; I'd knife-kill him on the spot.

A drop of water dangled precariously from Sap's chin as he darted glances across the faces staring at him. His

answer was taking too long—I knew he had to be wondering why I wanted to know, and why I had knowledge of
the Havelock cap. It quickly dawned on me that if he was
part of Tinbac's massacre, he wouldn't be dumb enough
to reveal it.

Sap answered, nodding his head as if to emphasize the
point. The droplet of water fell to the ground as he gave
me a smile. I'd seen that smile on bar girls trying to sell
Saigon tea.

"Him say abou one wee ago, Sar Brett."

I looked at Fayden, then Tuong. "Do you believe him?"
I asked, feeling a strong gust of wind-laced rain pelt my
back.

Tuong shrugged as a second gust of wind caused Sap
to fall backward off the rucksack we had him sitting on. I
leaned forward and grabbed his hands to pull him up.
Feeling the texture of his palm, I noticed it was uncom-
monly smooth; no callouses.

"Find out what Sap does, what his job is. Ask him how
long he's been fucking that girl."

A minute later Tuong said, "He same-same medic, Sar
Brett. And say him focking dat girl only abou two minute
before you—"

"No, no," I said, interrupting. "I don't want to know
how long he was fucking her now . . . or then. How long
has he been seeing her . . . you know? Days, weeks,
whatever?"

"Okay, I'm understan," Tuong assured me.

My question had a purpose. If he'd been slipping off
with the girl for any length of time, then she'd know if he
was gone yesterday. I planned to extract that information
from her during questioning to determine if Sap was lying
about not being with Tinbac's gang.

"Him be focking dat girl, name Chua, for many week
since time dae come dis place Na Dao."

Looking closer, I wondered why an attractive Hmong
girl would be enamoured with Sap. Besides being the en-

emy, he was skinny, had yellow teeth, and worse, he was a communist. I knew it was possible she feared for her life, but no one was holding a gun to her head when I encountered them. And her rhapsody of pleasure hadn't sounded like an act.

"Okay, Sap," I said, moving closer to him. "Tan-Pop! You know about Tan-Pop?" I blurted, looking for any sign in his eyes that might reveal fear or surprise. I caught him by the shoulder, seeing that he was about to topple backward again.

Clearly startled with my sudden question, he muttered a string of rapid-fire words, then tried to make a praying gesture again. I stood, slapping his hands away. "Don't give me that shit, Sapo!"

Fear flashed in his eyes, which was exactly what I wanted. Sap had been lured into a false sense of confidence by our civility. I'd decided to switch directly from at ease to double-time march.

"Sar Brett, him say—"

"I don't give a fuck what he said! Whatever it was, is bullshit!

"Ask him . . . no, tell him that I know he's lying. Tell him I'm going to rip-cut his fucking ears off and make him eat them if he doesn't get straight with me real fucking pronto!"

Tuong's dark eyes squinted at me in disbelief. It wasn't my intention to rattle Tuong, but I was glad his reaction had been spontaneous.

"Tell him, damn it!" I uttered, jabbing a finger at Sap.

Copying the gesture, Tuong turned and jabbed his finger at the prisoner, emphasizing my words. Sap's knees began to tremble—he quickly pressed them together.

As Tuong finished, I yanked the knife from my shoulder scabbard and took a fast step forward. "Lets hear it, Sapo! Now!"

Falling backward, his feet dug madly at the rocky surface as he tried to squirm away. He jabbered a full, automatic oration complete with snot-laced blood spilling over his upper lip onto his wagging tongue.

I caught a peripheral glimpse of Fayden moving to my side as I dropped to one knee, prodding my knife at Sap's quivering gullet. "It better be good, Sapo," I whispered loudly, moving my head to within inches of his shocked face.

"Sar Brett, no kill!" Tuong said touching my shoulder. "Him talk abou Tan-Pop."

Pulling away, I stood, turned, and stepped in front of Tuong. A chilling gust of wet wind slapped my face as I spoke. "What? What did he—" A scream halted me.

The piercing boom of a shot resounded in my ear. I whirled to see Sap's bloody skull cracked open like a ripe melon. "Damn it, Fayden," I mumbled. "Goddammit!"

"*Sat cong! Sat cong!*" he said, squatting, then spitting at the red-cloaked gore. "*Sat cong!*" he repeated.

I blamed myself for setting Fayden in motion. He'd seen me threaten to kill the prisoner, but he hadn't known it was a false act. There was nothing false about Fayden's action—he'd point-blank nailed Sap, and the look on Fayden's face showed no regret.

"Brett, Brett," Ski's labored voice traveled ahead of his hurried pace toward me. "What's hap . . . hoo . . . lee shit!" he murmured stopping in his tracks. Rain dribbled off the brim of his bush hat as he stared down at the dead Pat. "Holy . . . why did you—"

"Where's the girl?"

"She—she's with Lok. I—I thought you needed—"

"Get back there and wait for us; we're moving now!" I said, kicking Sap's limp legs away from my ruck and reaching to hoist it onto my shoulder.

"Tuong, get Rham and Phan and meet us over there. Hurry!" I jerked a nod toward the fading silhouette of Binkowski withdrawing into the rainy haze.

I didn't know if the rifle shot could have been heard in the village, but the chances were, it was. The heavy rain obscured some noise, but I was certain that the rock cliff had amplified the shot.

Moving with Fayden toward Ski's position, I made a mental tally. A total of five Pathet-Lao were now KIA; if they'd heard the shot in Na Dao and started missing Chua and the others, they'd be stirred up like a stick in a beehive.

When we reached Ski's position, I glanced at the girl. She was squatted—trembling. Water streaked over her grim face as if she knew her lover was dead and the same fate awaited her.

# Chapter 18

When Tuong, Rham, and Phan reached my position we asked Fayden to get us to a safe area.

During the translation between Fayden and Tuong I could tell that the Hmong didn't like the idea of withdrawing—it seemed that Fayden had killing on his mind and was ready and eager to march into Na Dao and start the show. My perception was center target; I knew it the minute Tuong turned to me.

"Sar Brett, him wan go Na Dao kill Pat-Lao. No wan run away."

"We're not retreating, damn it! We're playing it safe for now. Tell him!"

Seeing Fayden take a step toward the girl, I moved quickly between them. The clatter of thunder ignited my frustrated spirit—I was fed up with second-hand conversation. "You want go Na Dao . . . go! They'll break you in half with lead," I said, making an emphatic breaking motion with my clinched fists. "But if you stay with us you don't touch her! You got that!" I jabbed a pointed finger at the girl.

The Hmong stepped back, jerking his AK diagonally across his chest, frowning. I understood Fayden's anguish, but I didn't plan on hurling my team into a suicide mission, and I wasn't about to let the Hmong kill my last source of information.

Reaching down, I grasped the girl's tied hands and pulled her upward. "Tuong, tell him we're moving on with or without him.

"Rham, high ground, *dee*!"

Lunging toward me, Ski whispered, "Brett, I'll—I'll take care . . . I mean, handle the girl if you want me—"

"Negative. I'll take her. Let's go!"

As the team fell into position and moved into the rainy shroud of the jungle, I nudged the girl ahead of me, then glanced back to Fayden. He stood watching us fade into the undergrowth.

I didn't like leaving Fayden. Inwardly I hoped he'd come with us and get a grip on his emotions. In years past, I'd felt some of his hopeless sense of anger boiling in me when I'd lost my son. And, if I'd had a gun at the time, and someone to blame for my son's death, I would have used it on them, just as Fayden had done to Sap. But right now I couldn't let Fayden's shortened fuse blow what withering chance I still had to kill Tinbac and his scum-sucking cronies.

Twenty minutes into the dim jungle, Rham halted the team near the river we had paralleled earlier. A pile of teak timber was stacked on a nearby slope forty meters above the river. Rham found a small, woodcutter's lean-to at the edge of a cleared tree line. We stashed the extra rifles and LAWs inside the hut.

After leaving Tuong and the girl at the shelter, I took the remainder of the team and conducted a circular recon of the area. During the recon, I located and pointed out both a primary and an alternate rally point for use in the event we got hit and had to escape and evade.

I positioned Rham and Phan on the eastern slope to observe the village, and took Ski and Lok with me to the woodpile area where I told them to maintain surveillance on the river.

Before leaving to return to the hut, I looked at Ski's tired, water-streaked face, then glanced at my watch. "It's 1430 hours, partner. After I question this girl, Tuong and I will come relieve y'all and give you a chow break out of this rain," I said, quickly scanning the dark, windy sky.

"Roger," he replied quietly, with a hint of apathy in his voice. "Brett, listen . . . can you tell me what's going on? I mean . . . we, we've been tromping around this AO all day and well, you know I—"

I cracked a half-grin and tapped his shoulder. "Hang in there, partner. I know everybody's tired and hungry. I'll have Plan B worked out when I get some info from the girl."

Ski wiped his face and nodded halfheartedly. "That's great, but I'm not sure I ever knew what plan A was. And, shit, why did—did you have to kill that prisoner? Was he trying to—"

"Hold it, Ski," I said, feeling my eyes narrow. I remembered him asking about it at the scene, but I hadn't answered him. "I didn't kill the prisoner. Fayden did. He's got killing on his mind; right now he's a very loose cannon. Can't say I really blame him."

"Is that why you got hot with him back there a while ago?"

I shook my head. "No, not that so much. I just couldn't risk him killing the girl."

"She's real scared, you know," Arnold said sympathetically.

I stepped back. "Well good. She's got every right to be scared. Her lover's been killed and she's being dragged through the jungle not knowing if she's next. I want her scared. Maybe it'll help loosen her tongue."

"Her lover? Did you say her—"

"That's right. We caught 'em in the act—like a monkey fucking a football."

"You mean she and—and that, guy were—were doing

it in the, in this rain!'' he said, holding his hands wide apart and glancing skyward with a look of awe.

"No, not in the . . . they were in a shed,'' I answered, turning.

"Wait, Brett. I want to hear more. Were they—"

"Arnold, look. I don't have time to give you an after-action report.''

"Okay, okay, I understand. Do you want me to make our contact with Sunburst?''

"No, that can wait,'' I replied. Binkowski's expression asked why, but he didn't speak it and I decided not to volunteer an answer.

"Keep a sharp eye, partner,'' I said, walking away. I knew if we contacted Sunburst it was very likely they'd transmit an exfiltration order to us; I needed more time.

When I arrived at the lean-to, Tuong had removed the girl's gag. They were squatted facing each other, talking.

Seeing me approach, Tuong moved aside to provide some space beneath the small shelter. I took my ruck off and edged inside, noticing that the girl's expression didn't register the same fear it had before.

"Sar Brett,'' Tuong said, holding his open palm upward as if he was taking an oath. "I'm be talk wid dis *co*, Chua. I'm tink maybe she tell true not be Pat-Lao.''

Tuong only used his open hand gesture when he wanted to politely emphasize what he was saying. I glanced at Chua, then back at Tuong. "Okay, what makes you think that?'' I asked, turning to open the side pouch flap on my rucksack. I removed the half-full LRPR bag and unfolded it.

"It becau she tell me dat her Papasan being seek and dat man Sap him give her medi-sin to help Papasan.''

"Trading sex for medicine. Not the first time it's been done, I guess.''

I leaned and untied the rope binding her hands. "Ask her if she's hungry.''

Chua rubbed her wrists, then shyly accepted my rice bag and began to eat slowly.

I took off my soaked bush hat and wrung out the water. While I twisted the hat harder in my grip, I glanced at Tuong. "Right before Fayden nailed . . . the prisoner," I said, avoiding use of the name Sap so as not to alarm Chua, "you said he'd talked. I'd just questioned him about Tan-Pop. What did he say?"

As I straightened the damp hat and put it on, Tuong told me that Sap said an NVA patrol had passed through Na Dao several days ago with an American. He said the prisoner was tied and had a sandbag over his head. After the patrol departed, Sap had supposedly learned that the prisoner was the man called Tan-Pop. The NVA had only been in Na Dao briefly, and continued on eastward.

"Did he know where they were taking Tan-Pop?" I questioned, noticing Chua take an interest in our talk.

"Him no say," Tuong replied.

"Did he say if the prisoner was wearing civilian or military clothes?"

"Not say, Sar Brett. I'm tink Sap know more, but die befo can tell all."

I nodded, remembering the moment when Fayden dropped the curtain on our interrogation. But then, it was likely Sap didn't know much more about Tan-Pop than he'd told. Evidently the NVA, for reasons still unknown, had decided to take Abe Duell out of circulation.

If what Sap had divulged was true, it appeared that the NVA was taking Duell east toward the Ho Chi Minh trail; from there it was my guess they would transport him north to a prison facility. I still didn't have any idea why Duell had invoked their wrath, and, even more puzzling, was why they were keeping him alive. Based on the viability of Sap's last words, I decided there was nothing we could do except transmit the intel to SOG during our next contact which I'd put off until tomorrow.

As Chua nodded courteously and passed the LRPR bag

back to me, I could see her breast jostle beneath the wet shirt, a rip partially revealed one nipple.

"Tuong," I said, accepting the bag. "How about giving her your extra shirt, partner."

I'd begun requiring the team to carry an extra set of fatigues after a mission during which we got ripped to shreds by thicket thorns while being chased by hounds in a southern target area.

Tuong removed the shirt from his ruck and passed it to the girl. I set the empty LRPR bag aside and pulled the map from my pocket to divert attention to it while Chua changed into the dry shirt.

A moment later she smiled and nodded, giving us the customary, praying hands.

"Ask her if she knows why the Pats are in her village and if she saw the NVA bring an American through there recently."

After a lengthy exchange we determined that her story matched Sap's.

"Okay, ask if she knows of a Pat-Lao named Tinbac," I said, deliberately avoiding my hat-sketch routine.

Watching Chua's reply, I saw her make a hand gesture to her head as if describing a Havelock.

Tuong nodded as she talked, encouraging her to continue.

Opening my last LRPR, I looked at Tuong. "Keep her talking, partner," I said casually. "The more you can find out, the better."

I'd taken several bites when Tuong turned to me. "Sar Brett, she say many tings and say dat man Sap be gone yesser-day wid Tinbac."

I swallowed and looked directly at Chua. She kept her dark eyes leveled on mine. A tingle of exhilaration swept through me—however inadvertent, Sap had gotten what he deserved, but he deserved more. Now, I wished we could relive the moment and tell Sapo that we knew he was part of Tinbac's massacre; the flow of his blood would be sweetened somehow. I glanced at Tuong. "Did you tell her what Tinbac's gang did to Fayden's village?"

"No."

"Well, tell her. I want her to know about it all!" I stressed.

As Tuong spoke, I watched Chua's eyes. A slow curtain of sorrow came over her as if she'd known some of the victims. Finally she wept.

"I'm tell, Sar Brett," Tuong said quietly, as if he was remorseful at having been the instigator of her tears.

It didn't inspire me either, seeing Chua cry, but she needed to feel a cut. Enlisting her help was vital to my plan since we no longer had Fayden to assist us. However painful the experience, it was important to instill a sense of genuine purpose in the young girl, if I expected her to help.

As her tears subsided, she lifted the shirttail, wiping away the wet remnants of her grief.

"Tell her we need her help. Tell her tonight we are going to kill Tinbac and all the Pat-Lao we can."

"We do tonigh?" Tuong questioned.

"That's right. I'm not taking a chance on Tinbac getting transferred or anything else. I want that son-of-a-bitch! I want him now!"

Chua listened closely while Tuong emphasized our need. I'd decided to push for her cooperation while the horror story of the village massacre was still kicking around inside her. The other emotion that I knew had to be bothering her was the knowledge that she'd allowed a cold-blooded killer of Hmong to enter the sanctuary of her love.

I guessed Chua's age at about sixteen—she obviously wasn't some seasoned whore out screwing for fun and profit. The sacrifice had been for her father. If she would apply the same allegiance to our cause, then we had a chance to set up my hit on the Pathet-Lao—if she wouldn't, I'd be homesteading square one again.

# Chapter 19

When Tuong finished talking with Chua, he didn't give me any indication of encouragement. The lonely moan of wind whistling through a gap in the log shelter mingled with the beat of rain as Chua's contemplative eyes gazed out into the gray monsoon. I restrained my urge to break the silence and ask Tuong what he thought her answer would be. Instead, I took a last bite of my ration, then passed it to Tuong, indicating for him to finish it.

Moments later Chua looked at me, then spoke.

I peered anxiously at Tuong for decryption.

He took a small, ARVN poncho from his ruck and passed it to Chua. "Her say nee to go power her nose, Sar Brett."

"What? . . . oh, okay. Tell her not to go far," I muttered. "Power her nose" was a term the Cowboys had once heard me use in a Da Nang whorehouse. When a bar girl had left our table briefly, I'd commented that she must be going to powder her nose. When they saw the girl walk to the latrine, they immediately adopted the American term for themselves. I could never make them understand that it was an expression only applied to women. Even now, it sometimes caught me off guard when one of them would look up at me and say, "I'm go power my nose, Sar Brett."

I glanced at my watch as Tuong finished the ration: 1500 hours. Peering out in the direction of Chua's departure I asked, "How do we know she's coming back?"

"No sweat. Her be back. Her go look for sign," Tuong said, raising his eyebrows and pointing out into the rain.

I frowned. "Look for sign? I thought you said she needed to . . ." I leaned outward, scanning the area again.

"That what her say. But I'm knowing Hmong tink. Dae have question abou what to do abou sum-ting dae look for speer-ee to give sign. Dat what her do now."

"Well, that's fucking great! What if the spirits don't give her a damn sign? Then what? Shit!" I muttered. "These people have more superstitions than Binkowski and his grandmother put together!"

"Sar Brett, I being shur Chua find sign," he nodded.

"Why?" I asked, rubbing my five-day beard.

"Becau her having sum . . . many frien in Chung village and her know Chung, too, so her for shur will find sign becau it rhy ting to do."

"That's reassuring, babysan. But how long is it going to take for the spirit committee to transmit her a sign?"

Tuong shrugged. "Don know."

After a moment of thought a question hit me like a bucket of cold water in my face. "Tuong, you said Chua had friends in Chung's village. If that's true, then why didn't she know Fayden?"

"Her do know Fayden," he replied, knocking another mental domino over.

"Then . . . why, how, could Fayden have wanted to kill—"

"Becau Fayden mad like dog becau him knowing Chua be focking dat Pat-Lao, Sap. Him tink her change same-same Pat-Lao."

Tuong's explanation gave me a deeper insight on what was stirring Fayden. Now I was reasonably certain that once Fayden learned that Chua was going to help us, she'd be redeemed.

As more time passed, the wind began to subside leaving a vertical veil of rain. I went through an explanation of Tuong's and Chua's mission into Na Dao. I told him that, assuming he was right about Chua's help, he was to accompany her into the village and discreetly tell the elders that they had to leave tonight at 0200 hours and quietly proceed in small groups across the bridge, then on to Fayden's village. I felt that the key to getting the villagers to leave lay in convincing the elders that an attack on the Pathet-Lao was going to occur. I told Tuong to lie, if he had to, and tell the elders that Vang Pao had ordered them to cooperate.

"If the Vang Pao lie doesn't work, tell them an arc light, many bombs, are going to rain from the sky. Do and say whatever you have to, babysan," I stressed. "But make sure they agree to start unassing that village by 0200. No bags, no pots and pans, no pigs and chickens. Understand? It's got to be a silent exit or it won't work."

Tuong nodded. "I'm understan. Can asking ques-ton?"

"Shoot."

"How I'm going to tell you what dae say?"

I informed Tuong that I would move the team into the field shed at 2030 hours, and that he should meet us there by 2200 for final coordination.

"Your other job is to learn everything you can about that village before dark. I want to know exactly where the Pats billet, their guard positions, and particularly, I want to know if they have B-40s. And try to find out where that road is," I added, pulling the map from my pocket and edging closer to Tuong.

I pointed to the map contour lines representing a draw on the east side of Na Dao. "There's not a road shown here, but if the NVA are bringing in that artillery piece Sap told us about, then I know there has to be a road here someplace that will handle a truck. You're going to be a busy beaver, partner."

Tuong grinned. "Piece-a-cay, Sar Brett."

I winked while tucking my map away. "Okay, piece of cake. If you get those miracles accomplished, I'll sing and dance at your wedding. How's that?"

"No marry for me! I being playboy same-same you, Sar Brett."

"Whatever," I replied, taking a quick check of the time: 1515 hours. "It's taking Chua too long to find her sign. Let's see what's keeping her."

We found Chua beneath a teak. She was standing, facing the tree with only inches between her nose and the bark.

As we neared her, Tuong held a finger to his lips indicating silence. After a few moments of waiting and watching her mumble to the tree, I decided not to ask what the strange ritual symbolized.

Leaning toward Tuong, I whispered, "I'm going to check on Ski and give him and Lok a chow break. You stay with Chua. When she finishes talking to that fucking tree, take her back to the shelter. And, tell her what y'all have to do in the village tonight. Make sure she understands it all."

"Rogee."

Walking away, I glanced back and saw her arms reaching to hug the teak. "Incredible," I mumbled. "In fucking-credible."

Nearing the river area, I saw Binkowski and Lok huddled behind the log pile peering into the drizzle. As Lok scanned rearward he saw me approaching.

"How you holding up, partner," I whispered, moving to Ski's side.

"Okay . . . doesn't it ever stop raining out here?" Ski asked as he looked down, digging a finger into his muddy boot cleat to clear it.

"Roger, next February. Seen any movement out there?" I asked, looking down at the swollen river.

"Nothing except a buck. Where's Chua?"

"She's talking to a damn . . . she's with Tuong. Looks

like she may team up with us. You and Lok move on back
to the hut and eat. I'll stay here 'til you get back, then I'll
go give Pug and Phan a break.''

''That's great! I—I mean not about eating, but about the
girl. You know, I had this feeling about her right from the
start. I just knew she wasn't a communist. Maybe I'm
psychic, you know?''

''Arnold, go eat.''

As Ski and Lok moved away, I took a position behind
the logs and peered toward the river. Possibly I was being
too optimistic about Chua, but Tuong rarely said anything
that didn't turn out to be right, and he'd given a thumbs-
up on her.

Watching the murky path of limbs and leaves being
swept along in the dark river's strong current, my thoughts
centered on the possibility of the NVA arriving in Na Dao
before we had a chance to strike. Sap had indicated that
the arrival of the anti-aircraft gun was overdue.

If Chuck showed up, it was very likely it would only
be a small detachment. We could handle that—anything
more would bring up a punting situation.

The possibility of knocking out an AAA gun sweetened
the pot more.

I caught a glimpse of movement near the river. A dim
figure walked with a stoop like a cautious ape, taking a
few steps, then raising taller and turning as if looking
around. I yanked the binoculars from my side pocket,
quickly wiped the lenses, and focused on the creature
stalking through the tall grass abutting the riverbank. It
looked like a midget, but there was no mistaking the ominous form of his weapon—an M16.

# Chapter 20

The curtain of rain and tall grass made it difficult to see the details of the man's uniform. No head gear, no rucksack, short, cropped, black hair.

As he moved closer, I eased my rifle over the slanted log and checked my selector, making sure it was on semi-auto; a single head shot would take him out.

Pulling the field glasses slowly to my eyes, I tried again to examine the crouched figure.

He stopped and peered upward toward me, as if checking the log pile for danger. His sense of tactical discipline was somewhere between stupid and non-existent—he'd walked directly into a custom-tailored ambush zone. He'd exposed himself in clear view with no hard cover available and no withdrawal except into a rushing river, and now he was staring directly into my sights. Finally he turned and made an arm signal back toward the area he'd just traversed.

Within seconds, four men hurried through the grass toward the point man. I flipped my selector to rock and roll.

The men grouped around dumb-ass, talking. One soldier seemed to be chewing out the point man; his arm waved as if indicating his irritation.

There was something familiar about the stout man. I focused on his face—it was snaggletooth—Ha.

Scanning the area, I saw another portly man ambling through the grass toward the group like he was on a nature tour. He was taller than the others and appeared to be Caucasian. He wore a blue, rain jacket with the hood pulled over his head; no rifle, but he had a small matching backpack.

Initially I considered letting them pass without exposing our presence, but with Ha in the area, I decided not to risk the possibility of running into his potential ambush somewhere down the road—my Cowboys were carrying AKs and in this country that represented enemy.

Looking back at Ha, I saw him point upward toward my area as if telling dumb-ass to move to higher ground. As they advanced, I tucked my binoculars away, then positioned my bush hat over the front sights of my rifle and raised it slowly upward. I could have stood to signal Ha, but based on the ineptitude of the point man, I decided a cautious signal would be wiser.

Staying low, I watched their approach while oscillating my rifle in clear view.

Stopping abruptly, the small point man gaped, then dropped quickly to one knee and shouldered his rifle aiming directly at me.

"Oh shit," I mumbled, jutting my rifle up and down.

Ha's authoritative voice wafted through the rain. "Ho! Ho!"

Dumb-ass looked back briefly at Ha, but kept his rifle trained toward me.

As Ha emerged into view he grinned. "Hey, Cee-Cee-N, what you do? Fall down maybe?" He laughed, walking closer. I was glad Ha recognized my hat but could do without his wit.

Seeing the point man lower his rifle, I stood, clawing lumps of mud off my knees as Ha approached. I glanced at him, ignoring his ear-to-ear grin.

"Roger. That's right," I said, wringing my bush hat out and putting it on. "I fell down laughing."

Ha frowned. "What you laugh?"

I cracked a half-grin. "Well, at first I was laughing at
your point man there. He walked you right into my ambush. Then I started laughing at you when you brought
your whole team into my sights." I smiled at Ha. "Finally, I just fell down laughing."

"No problem. Him new man," he said, frowning and
nodding toward the point man. "Him what call, in training."

Easing my rifle sling down over my neck, I saw the
Caucasian striding toward us. "Yeah, no problem. I'll bet
your patrolling classes could hold their graduation ceremony in a phone booth!"

"What mean pho-boot?"

"Just a joke, Ha," I said, offering my hand to him.

Accepting my handshake firmly, Ha darted a look
around the log pile. "Where you team?"

"Back there," I answered, glancing rearward.

"Good afternoon, sir!" the Caucasian broke in with a
stern voice. He plodded forward, jutting his hand at me.
"I am Reverend Vandyke Kingston. And I must say, it is
good, very good, to meet a fellow American out here in
this . . . in this devil's wasteland. You may call me Vandyke. And what is your name, sir?"

"Yancy, Brett Yancy," I answered, feeling the smooth,
wet texture of his palm. Two curly patches of hair resem-
bling rusty steel wool arched over his gray eyes.

Kingston drew his hand away from mine, wiping the
traces of mud on his rain jacket. "And what is your func-
tion out here in—"

"In this devil's wasteland?" I interjected. "I'm not—"

"Him Cee-Cee-N. Look for Tan-Pop," Ha butted in.

I hadn't planned on revealing the nature of my mission,
primary or secondary, to Kingston—obviously Ha didn't
share my sense of discretion.

"Well, it appears everyone is searching for Mr. Duell,"
the Reverend announced, propping his hands on his hips

and looking out into the thinning mask of rain. "As for me, I have ultimate faith in God's will. You understand of course, that the Lord sometimes works in mysterious ways. If Abraham Duell is departed, it is no doubt God's will!" He finished his prophetic oration clasping his hands in front of his stomach and tilting his head downward.

Ha tossed a dubious glance at the reverend while lighting a cigarette. He then motioned for his men to fan out and provide security.

Judging from the tone and content of Kingston's words, I got the impression that although he knew Abraham Duell, he wasn't particularly enamored of him. I guessed that Duell's reportedly rough-cut style contrasted sharply with the reverend's attitude. And, the fact that Duell was nobody's lackey, could be an indicator that they'd locked horns once or twice.

"Ha, did you know Tan-Pop?" I asked casually.

"I'm knowing. Him good man. Do many good things for Hmong."

"How about you, reverend?"

Turning, he glanced down at Ha, then back to me. "Yes," he answered reluctantly. "I knew Abraham. He was a bit abrasive, profane at times . . . pontifical at times. But all in all, I'd have to agree with Ha's estimation. He was a fair man and he was slowly weaning the people away from opium cultivation.

"Abraham's problem was that he never accepted the Lord. He was always misquoting William Henley. He used to say, 'I am the master of my soul, captain of my fate.' "

Kingston raised his rusty eyebrows and pointed a finger upward. "Of course, you know he was out of context. Henley penned, 'I am the master of my fate, I am the captain of my soul,' which of course is only a flimsy rhetorical crutch for denying divine providence."

Kingston went on, it seemed he was priming his bagpipes for a full-blown sermon. After listening to his solemn explanation about divine providence, I decided it was nearing time to cut him off before he passed the collection plate. Up until now I'd avoided telling them about my abduction of prisoners or my planned attack on Na Dao as well as what I'd learned about Duell  Before tipping my hand I needed to get a tactful pulse check on how Ha would react to my plan—for all intents and purposes, here and now, Ha represented the sanctioned army of Laos. Although elimination of the enemy was his foremost mission, I knew it was possible that he could revoke my plan on the simple basis of not wanting to get involved with something which his general, Vang Pao, hadn't approved. It was important to avoid a pissing contest with Ha.

Ha could be helpful in the attack—I could use him to provide security and to assist the people during their movement to Fayden's village. Without knowing his disposition, however, I decided, at least for the moment, to rely on the old Special Forces proverb: "If you don't ask, they can't say no."

Interrupting Kingston's divine filibuster, I spoke sharply. "Okay, I understand, reverend. But how did you get linked up with Ha? Surely you're not the team chaplin."

"No, I am not! I am a Lutheran missionary. Ha is providing safe conduct for me from the village of Muong Kha to Tiong Cone where I hope to expand my ministry, now that . . . now that the warmongers have seen fit to level Muong Kha." Kingston sat down near Ha as if exhausted and bewildered by what he'd just revealed.

"Which warmongers leveled your village? You know there are several factions out here which qualify as war—"

"I am referring to the ultimate warmongers, of course!" he proclaimed, standing again. "The United States. They bombed the whole area up there, gave us ten hours to clear out. I still recall, with vivid clarity, those awful sounds in the distance; there wasn't even enough time to transport my piano."

As Kingston leaned forward on his knees, Ha tapped

his back. "No sweat. You buy get-tar next time. Easy to carry."

Ha's suggestion didn't improve the reverend's spirit. The look on Kingston's face almost made me sorry he'd lost his damn piano. I wasn't about to ask how he'd managed to get a piano out here in the first place.

I glanced at my watch: 1605. Ski and Lok would be returning soon. I needed a couple of important answers before they arrived.

Taking a canteen from my web gear, I passed it to the reverend along with a carefully-worded question. "The communists have allowed Duell to operate here for years. Why do you think they suddenly wanted him out of the picture?"

# Chapter 21

I sat down and waited while the reverend carefully wiped the mouth of the canteen and took a long drink.

"Thank you," he said, returning the canteen and studying me closer. "What is your . . . are you an officer or enlisted?"

I offered my water to Ha before answering. Ha declined, then stood and walked away toward one of his troops. "Be back. We have go soon."

"Sergeant," I said, tucking the canteen away.

Kingston sighed. "Yes, well . . . I considered the army when I graduated from the seminary. They offered me the rank of lieutenant if I joined."

"I'm sorry to hear that."

Kingston frowned. "What? You're sorry to hear that I didn't join up?"

"No . . . that they wanted to make you a lieutenant."

"Oh," he replied studiously. "I suppose you are right. It should have been at least an offer of captain."

It seemed Reverend Kingston had forgotten my original question or was trying to ignore it; either was unacceptable.

Making a slow scan of the area, I decided to nudge Kingston. "Did you forget about my question or are you just avoiding it?" My eyes stopped on his.

He squinted. "Yes, your question . . . no, I'm not avoiding your question. Basically, I was trying to ascertain your knowledge of economics. Did you join the army or were you drafted?"

Feeling my eyes narrow, I went ahead and answered his left field question. "I joined. All Special Forces personnel are volunteers—multi-level volunteers."

"Oh, well, good. I was wanting to determine if you could—"

"Look, reverend, I've had about sixty college hours if that's what's bugging you. So how about let's skip all this rhetorical badminton, okay?"

Vandyke was silent. He sat rigidly erect and tight-lipped, squeezing his right earlobe between his thumb and index finger. Then he leaned forward slightly and crossed his legs. He appeared to be trying to relax. "You . . . asked what I considered to be the reason Abraham, if I may quote you, was taken out of circulation . . . or perhaps killed by the communists after being ignored, rather, unbothered, for years.

"My personal feeling is that he has not been killed. Abducted yes; killed, definitely not. But why not killed?

"It's simply because he is a displaced god to the Hmong; the communists know that if they kill him they risk total alienation of the indigenous populace—the Hmong. That kind of news travels fast in these mountains. The Hmong would know if he were dead. So they, the communists, have only removed him. Supposedly it is temporary, until things get back to normal. The Hmong don't necessarily like it, but they can accept Abraham's POW status much easier than his death because they believe it is the spirits' will."

Glancing skyward and noticing that the rain had stopped, Kingston pulled his jacket hood off his near-balding head.

"Why wouldn't the Hmong just as easily accept the fact

that Duell had been killed?'' I asked. ''Seems feasible that they could chalk that up to the spirits' will too.''

Raising a finger emphatically, he responded. ''No! Because Duell is a non-combatant. For much the same reason that I haven't been killed, it is believed we walk with Divine protection.'' He smiled. ''Perhaps we do.''

I peered toward Ha and watched him squatting near his point man as if giving him instructions about something.

Looking back at the reverend, I said, ''Well, you're right about that. He's alive.''

''What? How do you know? How could you know—''

''Because I snatched a prisoner and interrogated him just a few hours ago. He said he'd seen Duell come through Na Dao recently with an NVA patrol, tied and hooded.''

''That's—that's amazing,'' Kingston exclaimed, uncrossing his legs and looking toward heaven as if to acknowledge the miracle. ''How do you know your man, your prisoner, was telling the truth? He could have been—''

''Because when a man believes he's about to die and thinks the truth will save him, he spits it out real fucking . . . real quick. That's why.''

''That's amaz . . . incredible. But how did you obtain a prisoner and where is he now?''

''Hold it. Before we jump to another lily pad here, how about us getting back on track. You've told me everything but why you think they snatched Duell. Why?''

Vandyke turned and looked toward Ha before speaking. It seemed that he was sensitive about Ha overhearing his explanation. Ha was walking toward another man in the distance.

Turning his attention back to me, Kingston raked a hand through his sparse, red hair. ''As you are no doubt aware, the basis for most wars is rooted in economics. This abhorrent war here in Southeast Asia is no different. Our country wants to explore the rich potential of oil here, as well as expand our global grip by positioning military bases here. There are sundry other reasons, but my point is that Abraham was beginning to upset an economic staple that has been in place here for centuries: opium, ya-ying they call it. The Chinese, the British, the French, the Japanese, the Vietnamese, and other nations have sought to exploit that staple for centuries. But only Abraham Duell had, quite literally, planted the apocalyptic seeds which are . . . were destined to bring about the end of opium trading.

"You see, Abraham was teaching the Hmong how to make a living, how to cultivate their fields and feed their families, without relying on the opium industry. Equally important, yet frightening to the communists, was the fact that Abraham was setting up schools to educate the Hmong. The communists, as you may not know, tax all French export of ya-ying and it has become a vital part of their continued economic ability to wage war in South Vietnam. There is a network of Frenchmen who come into these mountains each winter to buy the ya-ying harvest. It is popular knowledge that they are holdover deserters from the battle of Dien Bien Phu. A ruthless bunch, I'm told, although I've never met them, thank God!" Kingston said, turning to check on Ha.

Seeing that Ha was still kneeling near one of the troops, Vandyke then examined the dark sky. "It appears we have a brief respite from the showers," he announced, standing.

"Will you excuse me while I relieve myself?" he asked, walking back toward the grass line.

As Kingston strolled away, I focused on his detailed explanation. Everything he'd said seemed to fit the puzzle. It was a matter of economics—all of Duell's good intentions, however benevolent and self-sacrificing, were about to throw a monkey wrench into the North Vietnamese economy.

Although Duell's agriculture program did not yet pose a significant threat, it was obviously on the horizon of doing just that—the NVA had decided to nip sweet potatoes, soy beans, and corn in the bud before they became an irreversible part of Hmong cultivation.

As my thoughts centered on Kingston's dissertation, I began to feel a deeper admiration for Abe Duell. I could see how the Hmong had come to regard him as a God— within the recent history of their culture it seemed everyone had sought to exploit them; everyone except one man working for $65.00 a month. And now, even that God had been snatched away from the people who loved him.

The annoying thorn in my side was the fact that Kingston was starting to seem likable. He was a self-styled, pompous, condescending, religious ass who was out here gliding through wonderland like a hot-dog vendor at a ballpark, but reading between the lines, I heard what sounded like a genuine voice—a voice that admired Abe Duell.

As Vandyke ambled back toward me, he stopped abruptly and bent to examine something in the mud. Signaling me to his position, he spoke in a loud voice. "Come and look at this."

As I neared him, he pointed to the ground. "Let this be forewarning to you, Sergeant Yancy.

"See that track?" he asked, splashing water away from the vague impression. "There are definitely tigers in these mountains and I am told they are man-eaters!"

I nodded. "Roger. I've heard that. There are also Pathet-Lao in these mountains, so how about lowering your voice."

He stood, brushing his hands on his rain jacket. "The Pathet-Lao are not the real problem here, sergeant. If you ask me, they're little more than armed hoodlums. It's the North Vietnamese that are the problem in this beautiful country . . . them and your demonic bombs," he added, inspecting the sky as if anticipating an arc light any time. For a second it seemed he was daydreaming about his piano.

I glanced at him. "Just armed hoodlums, huh? Did Ha

tell you what they did to Fayden's vil—'' I stopped, then turned, walking away.

"Wait, Who's Fay . . . wait a moment. Wait, sergeant.''

Hearing Kingston's voice hurrying behind me, I plodded onward, not wanting to relive the moment or explain the horror.

"You—you were about to tell me—''

"Ask Ha. He'll tell you about—''

Suddenly a howling chorus of full automatic weapons fire shattered the still air.

Diving headlong over a stack of timber, I impacted with mud. Clawing and squirming, I twisted my body around and saw Kingston flying through the air toward me.

"Oh Jesus, sweet Jesus,'' he muttered, splattering into the mud beside me. Splinters of bullet-riddled bark spewed over us as I scrambled, trying to get my rifle into position.

"Oh God I'm—I'm wounded. I'm wounded,'' Kingston shouted.

Jabbing my rifle over a log, I triggered a long burst, then arose quickly to glimpse the area where the enemy fire seemed to be coming from.

Sporadic bursts from an AK popped in the area near the river, then I heard yelling as M-16 fire riveted from the far end of the log pile. It was Ha.

"Oh God, dear God please—please. Oh I'm bleeding. . . .''

"Where're you hit?'' I yelled, rolling to Kingston's side. He lay face forward with one hand clutching his buttocks.

M-16 fire crackled from behind us. I saw Binkowski and Lok sprinting toward me. Weapons blaring, they slid into position behind the piled timber.

"Stay down!'' I yelled, shoving Kingston's face back into the mud as he tried to rise.

I hammered another long burst, emptying my weapon. Jerking a fresh magazine from a pouch, I quickly reloaded and hit my bolt release, driving a ready round into the chamber. The enemy fire ceased.

"Brett, you okay?" Ski shouted.

"Roger. Did you get a fix on them?"

"Negative, but I think it came from across the river."

"Oh, God help me!" Kingston moaned.

"Who's he?" Ski exclaimed.

"Never mind. Keep us covered. And we got friendly troops at nine o'clock; don't fire in that direction!"

"Roger!" Ski answered, peering back toward the river.

I pulled Vandyke's hand away from his ass, trying to inspect his wound. Blood flow was sparse.

"What are you doing to me?" he whined. "Oh dear, dear sweet Jesus—"

"Shut up! You've been grazed across the ass," I said, opening a flap on the side of his backpack.

I yanked a wadded piece of cloth from the pouch, then ripped his pants and placed the cloth over the bloody spot on his underwear. "Hold this tight and don't get up," I said, taking his right hand and putting it on the cloth.

"Are we okay? Sweet Jesus. I don't want to die, please Lord."

"Calm down, damn it! You're okay! And stop calling me sweet Jesus," I said, trying to stay calm myself.

I rolled back into position, rising at eye level to peer over the splintered wood. "Anything, Ski?"

"Negative, partner."

"Lok? What we got?" I questioned.

"No see, Sar Brett."

"Hey, Yon-cee! How you do?" Ha yelled from somewhere.

"One wounded. How you?"

"Okee-doe-kee for me!"

"Who the hell's that?" Ski blurted.

"He's on our side."

After several silent minutes of waiting and watching Ha low-crawled to my position.

"All clear, I'm tink," he whispered.

"Yeah," I answered, noticing his mud-laced frown. "If it's all clear, why'd you crawl here?"

He grinned. "Not sure."

"Oh God, I can't—can't . . . I don't have feeling . . . my—my posterior feels numb," Kingston whined, rising abruptly.

I jammed my elbow into his back. "Goddammit, I said stay the fuck down! You're going to be all right."

"Do not take the Lord's name in vain!" he said assertively.

His commanding tone indicated he wasn't hurt as badly as he thought he was.

"Roger, reverend. Got it. Sorry," I answered, lifting my elbow off him. "Just stay down."

"Are you sure I'm okay? I think . . . I think I can feel blood . . . or, maybe it's feces on my hand. Can you tell which—"

"Probably both! Trust me. You've been shot in the best place anyone could get shot. You're going to be fine," I consoled again.

Kingston squirmed, trying to turn his head. "I caused this, didn't I? You told me not to talk so loud over there. I think we should pray and ask—"

"Listen, preacher," I said, leaning closer and gripping his shoulder. "I want you to lie still, keep your hand on your ass, and stay quiet! In that order, got it?"

"Yes, yes," he moaned. "I still think we should—"

"If you need to pray, then go at it. Just keep it quiet. Ski, I want you to crawl back and check on Tuong, then go check Pug and Phan. They're on the east end of that knoll beyond the lean-to.

"Lok, move down and scope out that river area. Stay low. They've probably moved on, but I want to make sure. And here, take my binoculars," I said, tugging them out of my side pocket.

Jagged plastic grated my palm. Looking down, I saw

that the right viewing unit had been shattered by a bullet. I gripped it, twisting and breaking it away, then passed the left half to Lok. "There. See if that works. It's better than nothing."

Lok held the expedient monocular to his eye. "Work okay."

As Ski and Lok crawled away, Ha nudged me. "I go wid him. Help look," he whispered while pointing at Lok.

"Negative. I want you to stay here for now. We need to talk about something. How do you feel about killing *beaucoup* Pat-Lao?"

# Chapter 22

Ha and I kept our eyes and rifles covering Lok while he moved slowly along the grassy area. Ha said he thought the weapons fire had come from a small Pat-Lao patrol located across the river. We figured that the patrol had heard Kingston's loud voice and decided to take a few shots at us—the volume of our return fire had evidently dulled their enthusiasm for a prolonged fire fight.

As we waited and watched, I gave Ha the fifty-cent pitch on my plan to hit the Pathet-Lao in Na Dao—I masked my spiel in such a way so as to make him think that the potential success of the operation depended on his participation. I told him that if he opted not to help me, I'd have to abort the hit.

Although I had no intention of aborting, I wanted Ha to believe that I would not be pursuing "unauthorized military action" without his approval and involvement.

I knew Kingston had to be tuned in to everything I was saying, but thus far he'd chosen not to interrupt me. When I finished outlining the basic concept of my operation, I glanced at Ha to check his reaction. His expression was contemplative.

Giving me a frowning smile, he asked, "You come here wid mission to find Tan-Pop. Why you now no look for Tan-Pop?"

Ha's question was a reasonable reflex. As a field team leader for Vang Pao, he understood compliance with mission requirements. In order to pacify Ha's concern about my mission requirement, I decided to go ahead and reveal the intel I'd gained from Sap and let him know that it was now my judgment that Tan-Pop was no longer in the AO.

After telling Ha about how I'd gained the intel from a prisoner, he nodded. Speaking softly, he asked, "Where this Pat-Lao preez-ner now?"

Looking him straight in the eye, I lied. "I killed him, he tried to escape. But there's a village girl that will help us. She's back up there with Tuong," I said, glancing to indicate the direction of the lean-to.

Studying my eyes, he stroked his chin, then nodded some more as if in deep thought. Although I'd mentioned Fayden's assistance in snatching the prisoner, I'd deliberately avoided the truth about Fayden's execution of the prisoner to prevent any potential criticism of him. As the local cache custodian, I reasoned that Fayden was subordinate to Ha—there was no sense dropping him in the grease.

He yawned, then slowly rotated his eyes over to me. "So, you mission *fini*. No Tan-Pop, you can go home, Cee-Cee-N. Why you wan stay here maybe die? Then I be one laughing!"

"His point is well made," Kingston sputtered. "If you have determined that your primary responsibility here is to no avail, then it seems ludicrous for you to stay. Oh! Oh!" he groaned painfully, while trying to roll over on his side.

I glanced at his mournful eyes, then back at Ha—they'd double-teamed me—telling them the truth wouldn't work because neither of them would understand my thirst for vengence. I really didn't give a damn what Kingston thought, but if I expected Ha to risk his life and the lives of his team, I needed to give him some viable reason, some realistic purpose to go out on a limb.

"Big man come," Ha whispered, pointing.

Turning, I saw the crouched figure of Binkowski hurrying toward us. "All clear, Brett. Tuong and Chua, okay," he said, kneeling to catch his breath. "But Rham wants you to come over there if you can. He says it looks like a truck is bringing in a humongous trailer or something down there. I looked but couldn't be sure. Seems weird. Why would—"

"That's good!" I snapped, cutting Ski off as a spark of imagination hit me like a muzzle flash. "Go down there and tell Lok to get back up here. I need the binocular. Go!"

Looking at Ha, I winked. "How would your boss, Vang Pao, feel if he knew you'd helped blow up a NVA anti-aircraft gun?"

He grinned. "Him like. Maybe give me pro-ocean."

I tapped his shoulder and smiled. "That's right. He'd give you a promotion. Well, that's exactly why I want to hit that village. I'd get a promotion too, for knocking out that gun! With your help, we'll both get fucking promoted!"

"Well, that's all fine and good, but how about me? I'm in no condition to be party to combative activity, nor would I if I could!" Kingston whined.

"That's okay, reverend, we'll get by without you. Your ass is going to be too sore to be walking for a day or so anyhow. I've got a nice, little, log bungalow up the hill where you can R and R for the night while Ha and I go to work.

"We'll carry you up there and tuck you in and you'll be fine." I said, tapping his ass with my rifle stock as I stood.

"Oh! Watch it, please. I'm very tender! And . . . I'm also worried about infection. Do you have any antiseptic?"

"Sure do," I answered. "And I've got something else

to assist your speedy recovery." I reached into my pocket and removed the small bottle of Ampicillin.

Handing the bottle to Kingston, I told him what it was, then added, "While Ha and I go to scope out that truck, I'll have Ski stay here and bandage your butt. With Ampicillin and rest, you'll be fine in no time. Then you can press on and expand your ministry like you said. How's that, reverend?"

Inspecting the bottle, Kingston mumbled, "I suppose I should rest before continuing the journey. It's painful, you know?"

"I can imagine. In fact, you're lucky to be alive." I said sympathetically while looking over at Ha. "You got a problem with the preacher here resting for a day while you're giving us a hand?"

"Not problem. But how you know for sure big gun come Na Dao?"

"That's what we're going to see now." I answered as Ski and Lok approached. I took my field-expedient monocular and instructed Binkowski to treat Vandyke's wound.

"Ski, ya'll hold this position until I get back," I said, preparing to move out.

"And what—what if you don't return?" Kingston whined.

I shrugged. "If we don't return, then it's like you said—it's God's will, reverend. Don't worry, you're in good hands with Sergeant Binkowski and Lok here."

Smiling at Ski, the reverend asked, "Sergeant Binkowski, what faith are you?"

"Catholic, sir."

"I see," Kingston murmured.

Moving slowly eastward across the steep terrain, we encountered two members of Ha's team. He instructed them to stay in place and maintain vigil.

When we neared Rham's position, he waved us forward.

He was squatted at the base of a tall, teak tree, peering out over the misty, green valley toward Na Dao.

"This man name Ha," I whispered to Pug. "Where's Phan?"

Pug grinned and pointed up. "Him dare. See *sung phong khong*," he said, using the Vietnamese words for anti-aircraft gun.

Looking, I could see Phan partially concealed within the foliage, beaming down at me.

Handing my rifle to Ha, I grabbed a bough, pulled myself upward, and climbed onto a limb near Phan. Crisp wind rustled through the wet leaves as I straddled a branch. Bending branches away to clear my view, I peered toward Na Dao. Through the haze, I could see a flurry of activity on the far eastern end of the village.

I took the monocular and centered my focus on the goings-on. I could see the broadside of a large truck which appeared to be similar in size to a U.S. 2½-ton vehicle. The back cargo area of the truck was covered with a wide, arcing, canvas canopy.

Looking toward the rear of the vehicle, I viewed the long, ominous barrel of the AAA gun angled skyward. I examined the barrel and saw the flared, megaphone-type muzzle that distinguished the 37mm artillery piece from other guns. The turret area was covered with plastic, and they'd rigged a canvas roof supported by thick, bamboo poles mounted to the frame of the weapon.

I counted six pith-helmeted NVA. There was a large cluster of Pats swarming around the gun like spectators at an armory open-house event. Scanning the enemy personnel, I saw one NVA surrounded by several Pats. The uniformed soldier was pointing up at the long barrel as if boasting about the capability of the weapon.

Suddenly I caught a glimpse of a square-shaped cap amidst the group. My pulse quickened—it was Tinbac Havelock! He was standing with his AK at sling-arms, smoking a cigarette.

Squinting at the skinny figure, I mumbled, "Enjoy your smoke Harry, it's one of your last, you glob of spit!"

"What say, Sar Brett?" Phan questioned.

"Nothing, partner," I answered. "How about getting down and let Ha come up here. I want him to see this."

At first Ha was reluctant to climb the tree. After some encouragement, he clambered upward and took the monocular as I handed it over to him. I needed to make sure he saw the goods I'd promised in order to stimulate his appetite for the game. I also wanted him to get a feel for the village layout and terrain before I started mapping out his role in the raid.

Although Ha had told me he was familiar with the area, I felt it was best for him to get a current target analysis in order to get his mind in sync with the tactical situation. Without Fayden, I'd have to rely on Ha's judgment and knowledge about the village area—specifically, any possible escape routes the Pathet-Lao might try to use.

Additional intel about the village would be supplied by Tuong and Chua when they rendezvoused with me at the tool hut.

Ha handed the field glass back to me and flipped me a thumbs up. "For sure, Vang Pao be happy we kill big gun."

As he climbed down, I took a last look at the cannon. The fact that they had not detached the gun from the truck indicated they planned to move it to another spot. Sap had told us they were supposed to dig an emplacement for the artillery piece, but I couldn't find or see any evidence or excavation. I reasoned that the heavy rains had either delayed the project or that they got lazy and decided to wait for the NVA gun crew to pick the emplacement location.

I descended the tree and handed my monocular to Phan. "You and Pug stay here and watch that village. If they move that gun, make sure you know where it goes. Roger?"

"Rogee, Sar Brett," Phan replied while studying the

broken half-binocular. He grinned and held it to his right eye, then turned in a circle as if making sure it worked.

I glanced at my watch; 1720 hours. "Pug, have y'all had any chow yet?"

He nodded while tapping his stomach. "We eat befo."

Turning to Ha I asked, "You need to see anymore?"

"No," he answered, giving me his gap-toothed grin. "I'm say like spec-shol-fors say, let do it! Kicking ass!"

# Chapter 23

Before leaving the observation area, I decided to take a moment in the presence of Phan and Rham and find out if Ha knew where the village bridge was located. During our earlier recon, Fayden had pointed out the general location, but foliage had obscured the view. Now I had a chance to test Ha's knowledge of the area.

Kneeling, I withdrew my knife and sketched a vague diagram of the village in the mud. "Gun here," I said, making an "X" on the east side of the village. "Where is the bridge?" I added, handing my knife to Ha as Phan and Rham peered over my shoulder.

Ha carefully etched a line which I took to understand represented the contour of the river. He then drew another line extending from the village across the airfield zone westerly toward the tributary.

"Breege here!" he announced, stabbing the knife into the mud.

Pulling the knife away, I touched the tip of the village area then back to the bridge. "How far from here to here?"

Frowning, Ha stroked his chin, then turned, looking around and back toward the route we'd traversed. "Maybe same same what we walk come dis place."

I estimated the distance at roughly 300 meters, then

glanced at Phan and Rham to make sure they knew and understood where the bridge was; both nodded.

"How big is this bridge?"

Ha stood and walked to a tree and held his arm several feet from it. "Like dis far. Three tree lay over water."

His gesture implied that the bridge was about five feet wide and simply constructed of three trees laid across the river.

"Okay, good. This is the way we're bringing the villagers out. From here," I said, pointing to the area depicting the bridge. "You will take the people on to Fayden's village, and I want you to stay with them until we get there. Any problem with that?"

"Not problem, but how you get pe-po to come, leave Na Dao? Maybe day no wan go, leave bone."

Ha's hard frown endorsed what I already knew was going to be a tough sales job for Tuong. I didn't know what Ha meant by the "leave bone," but figured it was his displaced English meaning "leave home." At this point, however, I did not want Ha thinking I had any doubts about the feasible concept of my plan.

I stood, wiped the muddy blade on the skirt of my poncho, and answered Ha while replacing my knife into the scabbard. "Those villagers will be there. Don't worry about that," I said, mustering a dramatized look of confidence.

"And, by the way, once they're across that bridge, we're blowing it to prevent any Pathet-Lao pursuit." I winked and added, "That is, if there're any of the son-of-a-bitches left when we get through with them!"

Stepping closer, Ha asked. "How you blow up breege?"

"C-four, shaped charge. That's how," I answered, looking at Pug. "That's your job, partner. I want that bridge rigged and ready before the villagers get there. Roger?"

"Rogee," Pug grinned.

In recent months Rham had become the apprentice team

demo-man. He liked to make explosions as much as Lok liked making rice wine. Pug exhibited an aptitude for working with C-4 that bordered on genius. He'd once fashioned an expedient conical-shaped charge using a bent can—he was inventive, careful, and quick.

"You have block cee-foe wid you?" Ha questioned.

"No, not blocks. But we have Claymores, and anyone with Claymores has C-four."

During team classes at camp, I'd shown the Cowboys how to dismantle a Claymore mine, remove the steel balls, and pry out the pliable, plastic explosive from the backing plate of the housing. In our current situation, Rham would remove the clay-like C-4, fashion a shaped charge, and insert a blasting cap. He'd then fasten the charge beneath the bridge, feed the Claymore detonation cord back to a covered position, and detonate the charge using the hand generator that came with the Claymore. I estimated there was adequate plastic explosive in one mine to easily knock out the small log bridge.

Leaving Pug and Phan to monitor the village, Ha and I headed back to Ski's position to transport the reverend up to the shelter. After that, we would begin preparation for the assault.

As we moved through the trees, thunder rumbled in the distance, signaling more rain. Stopping, a thought nudged me. I began to wonder why Ha and his team, including the reverend, hadn't been soaked from crossing the river when I'd encountered them. They'd been moving along the same route my team had taken when entering this zone, so they'd obviously had to cross the river.

Querying Ha about how he crossed the river, he told me there was a large, fallen, teak tree that spanned the river about one klick upstream. I made a mental note to use that crossing as our potential escape route if it became necessary.

During the brief stop, Ha told me he didn't like the idea of resettling the villagers at the site of the massacre. I assured him that it was only temporary, telling him that once he got the sixty-odd people there, he should try and convince them to let him take them on west toward the area controled by Vang Pao. My reasoning took into consideration the possibility that other Pathet-Lao forces could eventually reclaim the area and perform the same ruthless slaughter they'd conducted at Fayden's village.

If Ha was successful in persuading the people to go west rather than return to the village, then I'd request the CCN commander, Colonel Kahn, to schedule an arc light on Na Dao twenty-four hours after we exfiltrated—if the Pats wanted the area after an arc light, they'd have to contend with water-filled bomb craters the size of backyard swimming pools. Ha agreed to the idea, but didn't say he was optimistic about gaining approval from the elders.

As we moved on, I decided to tell Tuong to use the pre-planned arc light lie when dealing with the elders in order to reinforce the urgency of not returning. Reconsidering what had occured at Fayden's village, I now had no remorse about saying or doing whatever it took to get the villagers out of the Pathet-Lao grip—the same wanton butchery could occur there any time.

When we returned to Kingston, we found him in a prone position reading to Ski from the Bible.

Binkowski appeared elated to see us as if he was tired of the reverend's company.

"What did you find out?" Ski asked immediately. "Was it—"

"It's a thirty-seven alpha-alpha, alright, complete with crew and . . . where's Lok?" I asked, scanning the area.

"He's down by the river," Ski answered. "I checked on him just a while ago. Not a sign of those NVA."

"They weren't NVA, partner," I rebutted while taking my poncho off. "If they'd been NVA they'd have put a rocket down range on us post haste.

"Before I forget it, Ha told me about a fallen tree up

stream about a klick. If the shit hits the fan and I'm out of commission, I want you to use that as our primary E and E route."

Turning to Kingston, I told him we were going to lay him on the poncho and carry him up the hill.

"Splendid," he responded. "I feel it may begin to rain soon. I also want to compliment Sergeant Binkowski; he did a first rate job bandaging my . . . my gluteus maximus."

"Wonderful," I replied, looking at Ski. "Go signal Lok to get back in here. We're going to need his help on this."

By 1800 hours we'd transported Reverend Kingston up to his hobo recovery ward—the lean-to. After some brief introductions, we positioned the reverend in back of the hut near the extra rifles and LAWs.

Kingston took an immediate interest in Chua and got agitated when he learned she was a key player in my plan. "Surely you are not going to involve this child in your combative action!" he protested. "Perhaps it would be best if she remained here with me," he added.

"Not a chance, reverend," I answered, nodding for Tuong and Chua to follow me.

After taking Chua and Tuong a few steps away from the hut, I turned and looked at Tuong. "Is she with us or not?"

Smiling, Chua huddled near Tuong as he answered. "Her wid us, Sar Brett. Her find sign liking I'm say." He gave me that firm I-told-you-so look.

I smiled. "Number one. In a few minutes I'm going to take y'all on down to Rham's position. From there I'll be able to watch your entry into Na Dao."

Looking at Chua, I noticed that her eyes seemed to radiate an innocent glow of conviction, but I'd been deceived by Oriental eyes in the past—and right now I was about to entrust Tuong to someone I'd found consorting intimately with a communist; there was no way to determine if her professed allegiance to us was valid. Her story about helping her father could have been a cock-and-bull fabrication. I didn't like having to trust her, but there was no realistic alternative.

"What's your gut feeling about her, partner?" I asked quietly.

Tuong glanced first to Chua, then lifted his dark eyes toward mine. "I'm knowing you worry for me, Sar Brett. I'm knowing des pe-po, Hmong. Day good pe-po liking Montagnard," he answered, slipping his arm over Chua's shoulder. He smiled. "Dis girl x-cep-n-al, liking you say abou me."

I nodded. "Okay. But you remember this . . . there is nothing in this damn mission that's worth losing you!" I reached out, gently gripping his shoulder. "You'll be smack-dab in the tiger's jaws down there. The minute things don't look right, you get the fuck outta there! Got it?"

Tuong grasped my arm as if to emphasize the same feeling. "I gotting it!"

"Gotting it," Chua mimicked softly.

I smiled. If Chua was deceiving us, it was an Oscar-winning performance.

Turning, I nodded toward the river. "First rally point is a fallen tree, about a klick up-river from where we crossed. Second rally point is that cave Fayden took us to. If we get scattered we'll link up at one of those spots. Strict challenge and reply. Roger?"

"Rogee."

"Okay, let's move back to the hut. I want to go over some things with everybody, then we'll press on.

"You haven't seen Fayden around anywhere, have you?"

"No see."

As a light veil of rain begain falling, I assembled Ha, Lok, Tuong, Chua, and Ski in front of the lean-to and gave them a quick rundown of everyones' immediate requirements. I let them know that I would finalize my plans only after Tuong returned to the tool hut with the results of his recon at the village.

I told Ha that his primary job was to be located and ready to receive the villagers at the log bridge by 0200 hours. I added that after all of them were across the bridge he was to lead them on to the other village and wait for me there.

Looking at my watch, I said, "We might as well get synchronized here right now. You have a watch, don't you?"

Ha answered, reaching into his pocket. "Have here," he said, withdrawing an olive drab-banded watch similar to our team watches.

"Let's call it 1820 hours," I said, turning to insure that everyone was in sync. I advised Tuong to take his watch off his arm and keep it in his pocket while he was in the village.

Glancing at Ha's watch, I noticed that the crystal was cracked. A closer inspection revealed that the timepiece wasn't even working.

"How long since you used this?" I asked, taking it, winding it, then shaking it by my ear.

"Abou one mon, maybe," Ha answered.

"Lok, let Ha here borrow your watch, partner. You'll be with us, so you won't need it for now."

Making the watch transfer, I decided to show Ha the position of the hands to make sure he understood what he was looking for and exactly when he should expect the exodus of the villagers.

I spoke while pointing at the face of the watch. "When this long hand gets here, and the short one is here, that is when I'm expecting the villagers to start leaving. They'll be told to leave in small groups. They should be arriving at your location about—"

"About noon tomorrow!" Kingston butted in sharply.

"What?" I exclaimed, turning to look down at Vandyke.

Kingston smirked. "Listening to your plan it becomes glaringly evident that you, Sergeant Yancy, do not have the slightest comprehension or remotest understanding of Hmong sepulchral custom. In addition, you fail to realize the time it will require for the people to excavate all those ancestral, skeletal remains, pack them, and—"

"What the fuck are you talking about, Kingston?" I blurted, wishing it was his mouth that had taken the hit instead of his ass. "What the hell is, sep . . . What has that got to do with—"

"As it applies to your plan, everything! And, you may kindly dispense with the profane outburst, sergeant. I am not impressed with your inability to express—"

"Okay, okay! Got it. Now what are you talking about?"

"For your edification, the Hmong hold great esteem for their deceased. More importantly, it is believed that if they do not take good care of the skeletal remains of the deceased, they will invoke the wrath of their spirits. Twice a year, each tribe goes into the village burial grounds to exhume and clean the bones of their past family members. Then they replace the bones neatly and re-bury them." Kingston grinned. "You have a problem, sergeant, because those villagers will not want to leave their precious bones behind! They will be adamant about taking those bones."

I shoved my bush hat back off my brow, feeling the knotting grip of frustration. "That's incredible."

"Exactly," Kingston responded. "More realistically, it is flagrant. You should have seen them at Muong Kha when they learned we had to go. It was like a frenzy with them all hurrying into the burial grounds, digging, packing; we might have saved my piano except no one would help me. They were too busy exhuming bones!"

"Well, I understand it," Ski announced, stepping forward. "It's simply their superstition. And who knows, maybe they—"

"Arnold, how about getting those LAWs and rucks out

of there," I interrupted, pointing at the pile near King-ston.

"Him tell true. That what I'm say befo. Day no wan leave bone," Ha said, looking up at the rainy sky.

I glanced at Kingston, then turned to Tuong. "You've worked here with these people. Why didn't you tell me we were going to run into this . . . this?" I said sharply.

The second my words slipped out, I realized I was tak-ing my frustration out on Tuong. "Sorry, partner, what I mean is . . . do you have a recommendation? What can we do about it?"

Tuong shrugged. "Not knowing, Sar Brett. Maybe I can telling dem come back later for bone."

"Won't work!" Vandyke snapped. "Thou shalt not lie! How do you expect to win the hearts and souls of these people if you keep lying and deceiving them?"

Glaring at Kingston, I decided it was time to get away from his negative attitude before it started infecting every-one.

"We'll talk about this in a while, Tuong," I said, reach-ing to grip my ruck and swing it onto my shoulders. "As for you, reverend, I'll tell you this—if lying helps save the lives of those villagers, then I'll lie until my fucking tongue falls off. You see, reverend, winning their souls isn't worth a damn if they're dead, is it?"

Kingston got quiet again. After Ski and Lok put their rucks on, I gave Rham's pack to Ha to carry. Tuong took Phan's ruck while I gathered the four LAWs, passing two of them to Ski.

Mentally, I tallied that we had a total of eighteen Clay-mores. I'd send two Claymores with Rham when he went to the bridge area—I wanted him to have an extra, back-up mine just in case something malfunctioned on the first one.

"What are we gonna do with those extra CAR-15s?" Ski questioned, looking at the four weapons propped against the hut wall near Kingston.

Peering down, I replied, "We're going to leave those rifles with you, reverend. Do you know how to fire one of—"

"Yes!" he answered contemptuously. "But I assure you that I shall have nothing to do with instruments of the devil!"

I nodded. "Whatever you say, reverend. Just remember that tiger track you found down there. It would be tough trying to expand your ministry from inside a big cat's stomach.

"Let's move," I said, turning and motioning for Ha to lead out toward Rham and Phan's location. We'll see you sometime early tomorrow morning, reverend."

"Yancy, wait," Kingston pleaded softly. "You have given me your poncho, perhaps you should take my rain parka."

"Thanks, reverend, but blue's not my color." I stopped and looked back at him as he held his Bible up toward me.

"I'll say a prayer for you," he whispered, trying to smile.

I cracked a half grin. "Don't say any prayers for me . . . wouldn't want you getting struck by lighting. It wouldn't look good on your efficiency report. But you might say one for those villagers. You can pray that Tuong is able to talk them into leaving their bones in the bone yard."

# Chapter 24

The images of Tuong and Chua faded into the misty twilight as they ambled slowly down the slope toward the village of Na Dao.

Talking with them prior to their departure, I learned that the village graveyard was located in a meadow beyond the other side of the bridge—the bridge had been constructed to allow access to the burial grounds.

Although Chua was certain that the Shaman would insist on taking the bones with them as they left, the considerable distance of the grave site away from the village meant that the digging process would not alert the sleeping Pats.

The good news came when Chua told us that digging into the graves at night was forbidden because the spirit of darkness would enter the grave. I told Ha that when he got face to face with the Shaman, to try and convince him to keep the villagers moving and come back for the bones another time, when the spirit of darkness wasn't a problem.

I realized that I was essentially asking the Hmong team leader to do something that was against his cultural beliefs, but now, even if he was unsuccessful in getting them to leave the bones, it didn't matter—the important thing was that the people would be away from the village when my hammer came down on the Pats.

When the last glimpse of Tuong's silhouette disappeared, I moved my monocular to view the truck and the AAA. They were still in the same position as before.

As I dismounted the tree, Ski asked quickly, "Are they okay?"

"Roger. So far so good," I replied, checking the time. "It's 1910 hours. I'll be back by 2000. I'm going to move down and check out our route to the tool hut."

"But why? We know where it—"

"It'll be pitch dark when we head down there. I'm going to put out some road signs just to make sure we don't get lost," I answered with a whisper. There was no doubt in my mind that we could find the tool hut—the important thing was that we got there as expeditiously as possible so as to limit our exposure to any LPs the Pats might have put out.

"Road . . . signs, what?" Ski questioned, as I gathered up a dozen broken branches near the base of the tree.

Holding a foot-long section of branch before Ski, I stabbed it into the moist earth to demonstrate what I planned to do. "Placing these along our route will help us get through that area without taking a wrong turn."

"Do you want me to go with you, Brett?" Ski asked, looking at his watch.

"Negative. You go ahead and make a blind transmission to Moonbeam and request exfiltration tomorrow afternoon," I said, looking at the bleak sky. "Chances are they're not going to be able to get a chopper in here until this weather breaks, but give them the LZ grid anyhow. Make the message short and sweet, then get off the air. Copy, partner?"

"Copy, Brett."

"I'll use Boston-Beans challenge coming back in. Roger?"

"Roger. I'll answer with . . . submarine," Ski confirmed.

Before edging out from the concealment of the tree line,

I told Rham to begin preparing his expedient Claymore demolitions while he still had some light—I instructed him to prepare one primary and one back-up, then reminded him that he'd be moving out with Ha's team shortly after I returned.

Soft mud sucked at my boots as I walked, occasionally glancing at my wrist compass. Every twenty paces I jabbed a stick into the mud. The winds had calmed some, leaving the gray dusk shrouded with a chilling drizzle.

When I reached the elephant grass, I skirted it north-ward until I could see the dim, patched outline of the cleared field. Pulling the monocular to my eye, I scoped the zone at head level to the grass. The isolated tool hut protruded like the dark roof of a VW bug half-buried in mud. I estimated it was seventy meters, straight line distance, from my current position to the hut.

I poked in three sticks at the edge of the grass line as a turn guide, then removed my lensatic compass and took an azimuth to the hut. "Zero-niner-two," I murmured.

Moving on into the tall grass, I felt the heavy weight of mud caked to my boots. I knelt, clawed the thick muck away, then wiped my hands on the wet grass. As I pulled at the blades of grass, a prone figure caught my eye.

Easing my wet finger onto contoured, trigger steel, I slowly angled my rifle toward the figure and stepped cautiously closer. My eyes squinted, scanning what appeared to be a dead body.

A step closer revealed it was a dead Pathet-Lao. His throat had been slashed deeply, nearly severing the head which was bent backward in a grotesque arch. Machete, I guessed. There were no other cuts on the body and no sign of a struggle. Whoever hit him had blindsided the man, taking him down with the first stroke.

Checking the surrounding area, I saw the dead Pat's AK—it had been dismantled just as I'd done to the AKs at the ambush site, and that told me Fayden was still at work. I was glad he'd chosen the silent-kill method. I didn't know where he'd gotten a machete, but guessed the tool hut as the most likely place.

"Fayden," I said, softly looking out through the pale, green grass. "Fayden," I whispered louder, moving on through the rainy dusk.

No reply. Only the soft splatter of rain on my soaked shirt stirred the erie silence. A few paces further, I discovered another sprawled body—decapitated. The head was nowhere in sight. The slayer had stuffed a wad of elephant grass blades into the bloody neck stump. The grass protruded as if the body was sprouting a mangled crop of weeds. It appeared that Fayden was becoming a tunnel-vision psycho.

I'd seen men who'd became mesmerized by killing. They were like the Bengal carnivores that roamed this area— once they'd tasted human blood, smelled the fetid vapors of death, they were never the same again—perhaps I was that way. I knelt, remembering the warm, greasy flow of blood oozing through my fingers when I'd knife-killed an NVA soldier months ago.

Gazing down at weed-head, I smiled—Fayden's kill was righteous. I felt a cryptic flicker of envy, wishing the dead Pathet-Lao had been my prey, my retribution, my prize.

It was 2010 hours when I got back to the team. The pitch-black cloak of night, combined with the drizzle, had slowed my steps.

I hadn't found Fayden. I'd checked the area around both Pathet-Lao bodies, looking for a Havelock cap. None. The one Pat whose head was still partially attached was wearing the common head scarf. I didn't find the missing head, so I couldn't be sure if the body was Tinbac or not, but I reasoned that with the newly-arrived gun and training crew in Na Dao, Tinbac, a squad leader, would be in camp conferring with the NVA cadre.

Crouched beneath the dripping shelter of a tree, I used my red filter light to examine Rham's two shaped charges.

"Number one," I praised, tucking the charges back into the plastic bags.

Rham grinned, then took the bags and carefully placed them into his rucksack.

Turning to Ha, I asked. "Does your team have knives?"

"Having, yes," he answered while raising his shirt to reveal a bone-handled blade.

"Good. Your position will be on the other side of the bridge. You must be hidden in a place that will let you have a clear view of the bridge and also let you have access to the trail."

Ha frowned. "What mean asses?"

"Access . . . it means like entry, a quick way to—"

He smiled, "Okee-doe-kee, I'm knowing place having asses. Why need?"

"Because if a Pathet-Lao patrol comes down that trail headed back into the village any time around 0200," I said, touching my watch to remind him where the hands should be, "then you need to have your team ready to knife-kill them.

"We can't risk shots and we can't risk a patrol discovering the exit of the villagers. It would fuck everything up. Understand?"

Ha paused, stroking his chin. I was aware that asking him to avoid rifle fire created a higher level of jeopardy for his team, but it seemed the only viable alternative. I told Ha that Fayden was somewhere in the area killing Pats with a machete, and that it was possible that Fayden would, if he kept at it, eliminate much of the potential threat of Pat patrols and LPs.

"Fayden good man," Ha responded proudly. He then suggested that the better method of conducting a silent kill was with a crossbow.

After asking where they hoped to find crossbows, Ha said he would borrow them from the Hmong graveyard— I learned that Hmong warriors were buried with their crossbows atop their graves in order to ward off the intrusion of evil spirits.

Ha glanced at Pug's rucksack and asked, "Wha time Rham make boom?"

"As soon as the last villager is across the bridge and you have moved them out of the area. I figure everybody should be across and linked up with you by 0300." I reached and held the red glow of the light to my arm pointing at the three on the watch face.

I then told Rham that after he had blown the bridge he should catch up with the villagers' procession, accompany them, and wait for me at Fayden's village. "If for some reason," I stressed, looking at Rham, "the villagers don't want to leave the bones, don't worry about it. Get yourself on to Fayden's village because that's where we'll be in the morning.

"If everything turns to shit, meet us at the big cave. Roger?"

Rham nodded as Ha touched one of the LAWs. "Having question abou big gun?" Ha said eagerly.

"Go ahead."

"Wha time me kill big gun?" Ha asked, smiling.

It seemed Ha had missed something during the description-of-responsibilities process. "Ha," I replied with a courteous emphasis. "You are not going to kill the big gun. I'm going to do that when we strike the village. The strike force will be my team. We'll hit them as soon as Rham detonates, makes boom.

"Your job is to handle the villagers. Understand?"

I couldn't see Ha's face well in the darkness, but the long pause before he answered told me his enthusiasism was waning.

"Me . . . no kill . . . big gun?" he replied slowly. "No get pro-ocean."

I tapped his shoulder. "Don't worry about that, my friend. I'll make damn sure that Vang Pao knows it was your team that helped kill big gun. It's my bet that he'll give you a promotion.''

Ha nodded as if accepting my opinion. I couldn't be certain that Vang Pao would promote Ha, but it seemed reasonable enough, and I'd insure that the CIA got the word to General Pao once we returned to NKP.

Reaching into my rucksack, I withdrew two aerial star-cluster flares and handed one to Ha. ''Have you used these before? Do you know how they work?''

Watching Ha examine the ten-inch long silver tube indicated he was unfamiliar with star-cluster. ''Watch me,'' I said, removing the cap cover and inserting it on the base of the tube.

''After you put the cap on the bottom, you grip it like this,'' I said, holding the open end of the flare upward and outward. ''Then you hit it hard with your other hand on the bottom, like this,'' I instructed, making a striking gesture toward the base.

''When you hit it hard, it will shoot a big bullet about two hundred feet into the sky. After a second the bullet will explode and big pieces of bright light will scatter in the sky.

''The color I've given you is red. My color is green.''

Ha quickly armed the flare and held it out as if he was about to fire it.

''No. Not now, Ha!''

He stopped. ''When I do?''

''You do, you fire it only if your shit is in the wind, only if you need help bad. Understand?''

''I'm understan. Liking if we having bad trouble.''

''Roger. Now, if you see my green flare it will mean that I have had to abort . . . stop the mission.''

''Why you stop?''

I explained to Ha it was possible that Tuong might discover something that could change the plan. I didn't mention the possibility of the village elders refusing to leave, but it was my primary concern. I'd implemented the flare signal as a contingency to allow me to notify Ha if the villagers insisted on staying. I told Rham that if he saw my flare, not to blow the bridge.

I knew that if the villagers didn't want to budge, I couldn't risk an all-out strike on Na Dao and the certainty of civilian fatalities. If that fourth-down situation came up, I figured I could get in close enough to put a couple of LAWs down range on the anti-aircraft gun, then *didi mau*. I told Ha and Rham that if I had to settle for just hitting the gun, that I'd pop my signal flare just before destroying the AAA. That would prevent alerting the Pats prematurely.

"Brett, are you sure those flares will work in this rain?" Ski asked as I disarmed the flare and placed it in my rucksack.

"Roger, partner. The rain will extinguish them fast, but we'll still see the initial sky burst," I answered, checking the time; 2025 hours. I'd planned to be at the tool hut by 2030 hours, but the briefing with Ha had taken longer than expected.

"It's time to mount up, gents," I said, closing the flap on my ruck. A stout gust of wind raked through the trees as thunder echoed in the distance.

"One last question, Ha, before you head out. If you were trying to guess what escape route . . . where the Pat-Lao might run, where would it be?"

Ha turned and pointed into the pitch-black night as if I could see what he was talking about. "If Pat-Lao run, day go on same same row where big gun come."

"Roger. So you think they'd head due east down that road and through the pass toward highway seven?"

"For sewer. Dae go dat way to hi-wa seb-on."

"Okay, gang," I said, shaking Ha's hand. "Let's do it. Good luck, Ha. If everything goes good, we'll see you at Fayden's village in the morning."

Shaking Rham's hand, I said, "Partner, you keep your ass down. Understand?"

"Rogee, Sar Brett. I'm being okay. You do same same."

"Roger, and remember if this rain keeps up, to cover those Claymore clackers or there won't be any boom."

Rham smiled. "I making number-one boom. And when go home we go Da Nang make number-one boom boom wid *co*."

"That's a deal, partner. See you in the morning."

As Ha and Rham moved off into the dark drizzle to link up with his team, Ski whispered, "Brett, you told Ha if everything goes good we'll see them in the morning. Is that right?"

"That's right," I answered, shifting my ruck onto my back.

"Well, I'm only saying this because you always told me that if everything is going good, chances are it's a trap. Remember?"

Ignoring Ski, I turned to Lok and Phan. "Y'all ready?"

Lok flipped me a thumbs-up. "Ready. Let do it, Sar Brett."

"Me ready," Phan answered.

"Brett, did you hear what I—"

"I heard you, Arnold. Don't believe everything I say," I answered, leading out into the rain-laced darkness.

# Chapter 25

The aiming stake road signs I'd placed along our route proved effective in guiding our movement to the tool hut—in spite of the rain and ankle-deep mud, we made our approach to the backside of the hut in less than fifteen minutes.

I'd deliberately skirted around the bodies to prevent having to answer what I knew would be a barrage of questions from Ski.

Kneeling on the north side of the hut, I silently signaled Lok and Phan to stay in watch position while Ski and I moved in to check out the interior.

With my rifle at hip-firing level I eased the muzzle forward, using it to gently push the door flap aside. The steady drone of rain melted over my body as I stepped forward into the hushed mouth of darkness.

"Shit! What was that?" Ski uttered in an urgent whisper.

"What was what?"

"Something big just—just ran between my legs!"

"Probably a rat," I said, hearing the vague sound of screeches.

Lowering my rifle to rest on the sling, I pulled my flashlight out and moved the red funnel of light around the room. The screeching halted, but there was a strange odor mingled with the smells of wet earth and the dank stink of stale opium—it was different from the smells I'd encountered here earlier.

"Hold it, Brett!" Ski urged. "Move the light back over there. I thought I saw some . . . ho . . . ho, ho-leee shit! Oh fuck!" Ski stammered as my light froze on the gruesome carnage.

Ski coughed, "Is that wha, what I think—it—"

"Damn sure is. Here, hold the light. I'll get rid of it," I muttered, taking a deep breath.

"Hold that light steady, damn it!" I whispered loudly while yanking an empty burlap sack out of a basket. I reached forward and gripped the blood-matted hair of the head. I lifted it carefully up and off the hoe handle it was mounted on, then dropped it into the sack.

"Tell, Brett, tell me . . . that wasn't, isn't Fayden." Ski's voice trembled as I knotted the sack.

"It's not Fayden. It's one of his recent victims."

"But why would he put, put the head in here like that?"

I tossed the sack into a basket near Ski. "Shit, I don't know. Maybe he did it to scare any Pats that come out here to fuck."

"But, and . . . why is he . . . what is he trying to prove? Damn, I mean—"

"Hold it, Ski! Obviously Fayden's a little . . . well, a little pissed off."

"A little pissed off?" Binkowski cried, stepping away from the basket. "Shit—shit, I mean he's fucking nuts! Dangerous I mean."

"Maybe," I blurted, taking my flashlight from Ski. "But if you'd seen what they did to his little boy, to his wife, the whole village . . . If you'd seen the fucking dogs and chickens eating on their sprawled, bloody bodies, you'd think this was mild payback, amigo! Now go tell Lok and Phan to get in here."

Moments later, I sat outside, peering toward the village and watching jagged spears of blue lightning rip across the rainy sky. I'd borrowed Ski's poncho and told the team to try and get some Z's while I stood watch. We had a long night ahead of us and I wasn't sure I'd be able to give them much rest before we started moving again.

This was the first time since I had taken over as One-Zero that I'd had my team split up in three directions. I didn't like it and now I began to question my own judgment—was risking the loss of one of my comrades, my friends, worth trying to satisfy my thirst for revenge?

Looking out across the bleak, water-splotched field, I thought of Fayden. Slowly, I realized he wasn't going psycho at all. Somewhere out there he was moving with the stealth of a tiger—cleverly, methodically, doing all he could to help us. He was counting on us. I remembered sitting by Chung's muddy grave and thought about the pledge I'd made to Fayden's little boy. My wet hands gripped the barrel guard of my rifle. "They will pay," I murmured. "In a few hours they'll pay."

At 2010 I saw the silhouette of Lok emerge from the hut and creep toward me.

He squatted at my side, pulling his poncho hood up. "You wan I do, Sar Brett?" he whispered. "Maybe you sleep sum."

"No thanks, partner. Tuong should be back here by now," I answered, checking my watch again.

For the past hour something had been bothering me about the village. Now I suddenly got it. I stood and removed my modified binocular from my pocket. I focused on the village again.

No fires. There hadn't been one, single, cook fire since we began monitoring the village.

Lok stood. "Wha you see?"

"Nothing." I answered, lowering to sit on my ruck. "Tell me, babysan, why wouldn't the village have fires tonight? Any idea?"

Lok glanced toward the village, then squatted. "Don know, Sar Brett."

"Me neither," I said, slowly turning my head to scan the field.

I knew the rain hadn't prevented the villagers from making fires. The Hmong used covered, open-sided hooches to do their cooking in, and they were accustomed to functioning in a rainy environment.

Gradually, my concern for Tuong began to replace my preoccupation with the absence of fires.

At 2230 I decided it was time to move closer to try and check on Tuong. Standing, I whispered, "Lok, put this rucksack in the hut, partner. I'm going to move in and see what's up."

"You wan I go wid you?"

"Roger, you might as well," I answered, using the monocular again; seeing nothing again.

As Lok entered the hut with my ruck, I heard a faint voice in the distance. "Sunny-bee-ches. Sunny-bee-ches," the voice whispered loudly from behind me.

I turned, replying into the wet darkness, "Georgia peaches. Georgia peaches."

Within seconds, the crouched figure of Tuong trudged into view.

"You're late! I was about to . . . and why'd you come from that direction? I was expecting—"

Tuong moved closer. "Becau Pat-Lao having guard on dis side of village and—"

"Okay, okay. Where's Chua?"

"I'm tell her stay wid her papasan Him bad sick."

"Okay, let's get inside. I've got a dozen questions to ask and—" I stopped and smiled at my number-one Cowboy. "Damn, I'm glad to see you! I guess you might as well tell me what the verdict is now. Did they buy it or not?"

"Day buy, Sar Brett. Day happy we come kill Pat-Lao. But I'm nee tell more becau—"

"Outstanding! Out-fucking-standing! Tell me the rest inside."

After posting Lok and Phan on guard, we lit a heat tab and Tuong began unfolding the results of his recon. He said that with the exception of a few guards scattered around the village, all the Pat-Lao were gathered at a large hooch on the east side of Na Dao.

He learned that the NVA cadre were conducting a long class on the anti-aircraft gun. The rain, and absence of enemy movement within the village, allowed him and Chua to move about freely. He'd drawn a rough outline of the village, noting the guard positions and the enemy hooch billeting area.

"This is great, babysan," I announced, scanning the red glow of light across his sketch. "You deserve a "pro-ocean" as Ha would say."

"No for me. I'm liking no for me," Tuong rebutted while sniffing the air. "Wha smell number ten? You far, Skee?" Tuong jested.

"I'll tell you what smells. That damn head over there in that basket. That's what," Ski snapped.

"Wha head?"

"Never mind that," I interrupted. "It's just some spare body parts. By the way, did you see or hear anything about Fayden?"

"No see. No hear."

"Okay. Do you know why there's no fires in the village tonight?"

"Yes. Pat-Lao say making no fire. I'm tink day no wan airplane to see big gun, maybe shoo rocket at big gun."

"That's exactly it!" I replied. "It's just a simple precautionary blackout until they get that gun emplacement dug and the gun concealed."

It was apparent that the presence of NVA in camp was making a tactical situation considerably more disciplined. Right now, the low cloud ceiling would prevent anything but a kamikazi from getting in here, but apparently the NVA weren't taking any chances.

"Sar Brett. Having one problem."

"Shoot. What?"

"Liking I'm say befo, Chua her papasan *beaucoup* sick. No can walk. Some pe-po, maybe foe, be having carry him, go slow to breege."

"How about if I go in and carry him? I'm good at that," Ski chimed. "I really wouldn't mind getting out of this place for a while."

"Ski, in that village you'd stick out like a tent pole in a parachute. Besides, I'm going to need you as a LAW gunner."

"Sar Brett, I'm tink Chua, me can do carry papasan and maybe get sum mamasan can helping."

I didn't like the idea of sending Tuong back into the village, but in spite of my reservations it seemed the best alternative and it would allow me to incorporate some well placed demolitions.

"Well, try it your way, Tuong, but I don't want you going too far out on a limb. Understand?"

"Rogee."

"The villagers will be moving out in small groups. You can ease back in there at zero-one. Okay, now tell me about these guards. Are they roving or stationary?"

"Dae stay one place. Sit and watch."

There was no way to determine when they'd rotate the guard shifts, but I was glad to hear they were stationary. It was my guess that the guard shifts would be rotated at midnight. I knew that if the Pats had had a late night training class, the chances were good that most of them would be sleeping like logs for the remainder of the night.

Tuong mentioned that there was one guard stationed on the west end of the village. He felt he could take him out easily with a knife kill, then drag the body into a hut—that would clear the primary exit for the villagers.

For the next half-hour we studied the village layout and

determined the best spots for the Claymore placements. I
planned to use twelve of my remaining sixteen mines, saving four of them for any potential E and E requirements.

The primary enemy billeting area was comprised of four
large hooches located on the east end of the village. They
were positioned between the AAA and two other huts, one
of which was occupied by Chua and her father.

Reviewing the situation, I decided to send Lok and Phan
in with Tuong. My reasoning took into consideration that
if he got into some trouble, at least he'd have some fire
power with him. In addition, I planned to use Phan and
Lok to set and detonate some interior village Claymores.

"Listen close," I stressed, looking at the blue glow of
light reflecting off Tuong's face, "because you'll be in-
structing Phan and Lok on what to do when you get back
into that village.

"I'm sending six Claymores in with y'all. I want you
to position them just inside the thatch walls of these
hooches," I said, pointing to the sketch of Chua's hut and
the adjacent hut. "Three Claymores inside each hooch
facing the enemy hooches."

I explained that after he departed, helping carry Chua's
father, that Phan and Lok were to remain positioned in
the hooches, ready to fire the Claymores.

"Have Phan and Lok cut a small opening at the base of
the thatch walls and make sure they build up a dirt mound
behind each mine to counter the back blast. Tell them that
when they hear Rham's bridge explosion, they are to wait
a few seconds, then detonate their mines."

"How long dae wait?"

"Tell them to count to ten, *muoi*, and then detonate."

"I see," Ski exclaimed. "That'll mean that any Pats
running out of the hooches will be—"

"Running straight into point blank annihilation!" I said.

Ski reached to touch the sketch of the AAA. "What if
they come out headed toward this?"

"Some of them will. That's when we do our thing, partner. You and I will be positioned over here on this knoll about forty meters from the gun. As soon as the Pats start to beat feet into this open area, we'll put two LAWs downrange on that thirty-seven. Then we'll blow out Claymores . . . six of them!''

''Sar Brett, wha Lok, Phan do when fini?''

''Tell them that as soon as they detonate those Claymores to beat feet out of there and *didi mau* back up to the tree area where we were when you left. Ski and I will link up with them there.

''With their AK's and magazine vests they'll look like Pats so they shouldn't encounter enemy fire. If they run into any Pats, tell them it's open season, blow 'em away and keep on booking.''

I told Tuong that he should link up with Rham and accompany him on to Fayden's village. I then asked, ''How bad is Chua's papasan?''

''Him bad sick,'' Tuong frowned.

''Okay, tell Chua that if y'all can get him on to Fayden's village, I'll try and take her and her father out with us tomorrow afternoon when we exfil. There's a hospital at NKP and I'll make sure he gets some medical attention. Roger?''

''Sar Brett, you number focking one! X-cep-n-al!''

''I can't promise we'll get him out with us. That will depend on the chopper crew, but they're pretty good about going the extra mile. We'll be exfilled by Jolly Green so there'll be no weight problem. Keep in mind that we may have to wait 'til this weather breaks until they can even get in to us.''

Turning toward the team rucks, I said, ''Now let's get these Claymores divided up and primed. Also, gents, once we exit this hut, this place is off limits. I don't want anyone coming back here. Copy?''

''Don't worry about me,'' Ski muttered. ''I don't like this place anyhow.''

# Chapter 26

After streaking our faces with charcoal camo-stick, we divided and primed the mines. I then pulled Lok and Phan in and went over their actions at the objective with them while Ski stood watch outside.

As we carefully wrapped each Claymore hand generator in plastic, it occurred to me that the optimum target opportunity would be to move in and nail the bastards while they were all in their night training class, but I couldn't be sure when the class would end—possibly it already had. I decided not to roll out the red carpet for Murphy.

By midnight the Cowboys were ready to make their insert into Na Dao. The rain had become heavier—it was a mixed boon. The rain would help mask our movement, but it would also mask the enemy and make our trek to the eastern knoll much tougher.

"Okay, gang," I said, as the trio prepared to head out. "This hut is now off limits. Don't even think about coming back here.

"Tuong, once you get Chua's papasan across the bridge, try to help Ha convince them to keep going. He may run into trouble with Shaman and the bone problem."

"Rogee. I'm tink dae no be problem. Dae wan get away Pat-Lao."

"Alright, y'all be cool in there. I don't want any of you

184

to get nailed tonight." I cracked a grin and reached my
hands out to grip Lok and Phan's shoulders. "You know,
there's too much paperwork for me to do if you get
nailed."

"Pap-wurk number-focking-ten!" Lok piped. "We be
cool."

Turning to the windblown door flap, I yanked it aside.

*"Sat cong!"* A voice blurted square into my face.

Jumping back, I jutted my rifle at the grass blotched
figure.

"Fayden!" Tuong proclaimed.

The Hmong grinned. He was caked with mud. Grass
was strewn over his torso—he looked like the "Abomi-
nable" scarecrow.

"How the fuck did he get past Ski?" I muttered to
myself, moving backward to let him in. His eyes radiated
a caustic, penetrating glow.

He was carrying a crossbow. A wooden, sheathed machete hung by his side, strapped to his waist with a leather
sash.

Taking a deep breath, I lowered my rifle. It was apparent that between his FX costume and the heavy rain, Fayden had had no problem slipping by Ski or anyone else.

I nodded. *"Nhajong*, Fayden. Good to see you. Tuong,
tell him we're ready to hit Na Dao. And tell him that I
don't have any heartburn about him killing Sap."

I had no idea where Fayden's AK was or why he had
decided to contact us, but I wasn't about to let him trip us
up now that we were on the brink of launching our hit.

Tuong talked quietly with Fayden as I stood listening
and watching the blue glow of heat tab light dance over
the Hmong's face. Several times Fayden repeated what had
evidently become his new favorite motto, *"Sat Cong."*

If my count was correct, I comfirmed that Fayden had
killed seven Pathet-Lao, and probably more. I planned to
rely on Tuong's judgment of Fayden's current use to us.

If Tuong determined that Fayden was a loose cannon,

slash crossbow, then we had a new hurdle to leap—I couldn't, in good conscience, knock him out and tie him up while we pressed on with the mission, because that would leave him vulnerable to any Pats who might discover him here in the tool hut. On the other hand, I couldn't let him run stark-raving loose into the village and risk him throwing a rock into the hornets before we tripped our trap.

I'd already determined that Fayden was doing what he could to help us—the presence of a crossbow and machete meant that he'd reverted to silent kill tactics. My gut instinct was that the Hmong warrior knew we were getting ready to hit, and wanted to be included.

"Sar Brett, him ask how you like head him put here?"
I tried to smile. "Wonderful. Tell him it was fucking wonderful. Tell him I liked it so much I put it in that sack to save as a souvenir. But find out if he's ready to go by the rules. I need to know, Tuong, and we don't have all night to stand around trying to find out!"

Tuong nodded grimly, then began talking with Fayden again. Moments later, Tuong relayed that Fayden was ready to help and that he wanted to accompany the trio into Na Dao. He also informed us that he'd killed ten Pats so far tonight.

"Well," I replied, trying to keep my expression passive. "What's your feeling? Can we trust him to play it our way or not?"

Tuong's pause told me that he couldn't be certain, even before he spoke it. "I'm . . . tink maybe him be okay, Sar Brett."

"Maybe's not good enough, partner. I can't risk it!"

"Sar Brett, him could helping carry papasan," Tuong shrugged. "I'm nee help."

I squinted. "Does he firmly understand that Chua is helping us and that she is not Pat-Lao?"

"Rogee. I'm already tell. And him know becau him see me, Chua go Na Dao to-ged-er."

"Okay, okay. But you make sure. . . ." I stopped and got eye to eye with Fayden. "Him in charge," I said, darting a look at Tuong. "You do what he says and only what he says.

"Tell him just like that, Tuong. No killing unless you say so!"

With our rifles readied, Ski and I lay stretched across the grassy tool hut watching the quartet move slowly out through the cloak of rain toward the village.

Heavy drops pelted my body. I chewed my gum harder, trying to ward off the nagging, monsoon chill.

"Getting cold," Ski whispered.

"Roger. We'll be moving soon. As soon as they're out of sight we'll head on over to . . ."

Suddenly my eyes caught a peripheral glimpse of something in the veil of rain.

"Movement. Two o'clock." I said softly.

"What?"

"Don't know, but it's . . . it looks . . . shit! It's a fucking Bengal."

"Bengal! You mean a . . . okay, okay, I see it too," Ski whispered turning his CAR-15 toward the tiger.

"Don't fire."

The animal stopped thirty meters away, as if sensing our presence. Slowly it turned without the slightest display of intimidation and moved casually away toward the western grass line.

Seconds later it was out of view.

"It's gone," I said, raising to my knees.

"Yeah, but for how long?" Ski chattered, while keeping his rifle focused into the darkness.

"Let's get our rucksacks and *didi mau*."

"I'm with you, partner. Like I said, I don't like this place anyhow."

If Fayden wasn't exaggerating about the volume of his recent kills in the area, I figured that the local cats must

be well fed by now. At least I hoped they weren't trying
to pig out on the homo sapien menu.

Ski was carrying two LAWs and the Claymore rucksack
and I was carrying two LAWs and the radio rucksack; we
moved northeast through the muddy field. We reached the
grass line within minutes, then held our position momen-
tarily while staring back into the field making sure we
hadn't been pursued by anything.

Boots caked heavy with mud, we plodded onward out
of the grass and up into the heavily-forested area above
the knoll. I estimated we were about 100 meters from the
AAA gun area, but couldn't be sure—the rain was like a
solid, black curtain. The only glimpse of distant vision we
got was when a flicker of lightning illuminated the sky.

Using my monocular with a hand shielding my brow, I
saw the vague outline of the canopied gun through flashes
of blue lightning.

"Looks like ninety meters or more, Ski," I said, handing my field glass over to him, then trying to view the face
of my watch.

Finally I pulled out my flashlight to scan the crystal with
the red glow. "It's almost 0100. We've got about two hours
'til showtime. Check out the whole area down there. We're
going to place our Claymores at the forward edge of that
grassy knoll. See it?"

"I can't see anything but rain," Ski muttered.

"You have to keep your eye glued to it until a flash of
light . . . there, see. You'll only get quick glimpses," I
said, as the sky flickered pale blue.

"Oh . . . yeah, I see. Didn't you say there was a road
down there somewhere?"

"Roger. We can't see it from here. It's on the other side
of the knoll. You'll see it when we move down to that
area."

"Okay, I'll take your word for it, but I can't see it!"

"That's what I just said, Arnold. You can't see it from
here . . . don't even try. Just familiarize yourself with the

area, then concentrate on that gun. That's our first target, then we'll blow our Claymores."

I pulled out a foil-wrapped candy bar and ate chocolate and rainwater while Ski continued to study the terrain.

Ski muttered while keeping the monocular to his eye. "I'm getting the hang of this now. The trick is to wait until the lightning flashes, then you get a glimpse of—"

"That's what I just told . . . never mind."

"Every so often I can see the hazy form of houses beyond the side of the big gun."

"Roger, those are the enemy hooches, and on the other side of them is where Lok and Phan are positioning their Claymore; facing the enemy hooches.

"Ten seconds after Pug blows the bridge, Lok and Phan will trigger their Claymores," I told Ski, adding it was my guess that any Pats that were still alive after that would think an attack was coming from the west.

I was reasonably certain that they would run east, as Ha had speculated, or try to take temporary cover behind the knoll to defend the AAA—in either case they'd be scampering right into our Claymore hellfire.

I knew that Tinbac would be somewhere in the confused rush if he wasn't cut down by the six Claymores that Phan and Lok fired—I hoped I would have the sweet pleasure of obliterating him with my Claymore blast.

"Brett," Ski whispered, pulling the monocular away from his eye. "Is this what they call a target-of-opportunity?"

Taking the glass, I rogered Ski's question, then continued my observation of the village.

"Why do they call this area the Plain Of Jars?" Ski questioned. "It's not a plain, it's mountainous."

Pulling the monocular away, I looked over at Binkowski, wondering why the sudden burst of curiosity.

"You're right. It's not. All I know is that they've found big, clay jars all around this region dating back over seven hundred years to the time of Genghis Khan. Ask Kingston about it when we get back. He probably knows.''

Ski chuckled. ''Kingston. He's a funny kind of guy, isn't he?''

''Hilarious.''

''That little Chua is sure a fox. I wonder how old she is?'' Ski said, leapfrogging to another topic.

I turned, trying to see his face. ''Partner, you've developed a rapid fire load of curiosity tonight. Why?''

''Don't know. I guess maybe I'm trying to get my mind off what's coming. You said there were about sixty Pats down there. Assuming Lok and Phan's Claymores take out half of them, that still leaves thirty for you and me . . . roughly thirty. Right?''

''That's about right.''

''Well that's fifteen to one on you and me, not to mention those extra NVA.''

I turned to study the village again. ''Seems fair. You're right about little Chua. She is a fox. I'd guess her at about sixteen, maybe seventeen.''

''Why'd you ever decide to join the army? Fun, travel, adventure . . . what?''

# Chapter 27

By 0235, Ski and I had moved down and positioned our mines. We lay prone on the grassy crest of the knoll less than fifty meters from the truck and gun. Somehow the big gun seemed more ominous in the closer perspective. The area was unusually quiet, except for the unrelenting drone of the storm punctuated by occasional thunder and lightning.

We'd routed the Claymore detonation lines back to our center position, keeping the hand generators inside Ski's rucksack which we'd placed on the ground between us.

I'd given Ski a brief refresher class on LAW firing, but couldn't be certain how he'd do. The M72 Light-Anti-Armor-Weapon had a maximum effective range of 300 meters and supposedly could penetrate ten inches of armor—the effectiveness of the weapon moved into the category of myth after one Soviet tank took nine LAW hits at the siege of Lang Vei and kept coming.

But we weren't firing at tanks and we only had a target range of about fifty meters—I figured that with two shots each, one of us had to hit the the AAA. Inwardly, I now wished I'd opted to bring an M-79. Commonly Rham was our M-79 carrier, but on this mission, a supposed "easy stroll in the woods," I'd decided to allow Rham to carry a rifle.

"Brett, look there behind that—that turret area." Ski whispered, handing me the binocular. "Looks like somebody sitting in there."

Taking the scope, I focused beneath the makeshift canopy they'd rigged over the gun and peered into the turret area. Wind lashed at the plastic covering, but clearly there was a small man sitting in the gunner's seat right beside the elevation wheel. He was slumped with his head tilted downward as if he was asleep.

"Roger, roger. He's not NVA. No pith helmet," I murmured quietly while noticing his AK laying across his lap.

I didn't know why we hadn't spotted the guard earlier while placing our mines, but was glad he'd nodded out on guard duty.

Easing my focus toward the village huts, I looked for signs of movement. The interior of the village was blocked from view by the enemy hooches. I estimated that by now the village should be clear of civilians; it was nearing 0300 hours.

I tucked my scope away, then removed four M-26 frag grenades from my web gear and loosened the pins for easy pull. I placed the grenades by my rucksack.

Watching me, Ski whispered. "You want me to get some grenades out too?"

"Negative. This'll be all we have time for. Go ahead and arm your LAWs. Do it quietly," I whispered. "Remember, when you pull those sections apart they make a loud click if you do it fast or try to force it."

"Roger," Ski replied softly while rolling to one side and picking up his two LAWs.

"Gently," I coached, as Binkowski carefully removed the end covers. He slid the sections apart, barely producing a faint click as the tubular sections locked into place. He then pushed the safety handle forward and raised the rear sights.

Once we'd armed the LAWs, we covered them with a poncho.

I pulled my CAR-15 up into firing position and took a bead on Rip-Van-Pat-Lao sitting in the gunner's seat. I'd decided that he had to be taken out immediately after Rham's bridge explosion woke him—otherwise he'd be a live-fire contender.

"What are you doing?" Ski questioned.

"When that bridge blows I'm putting that guard into permanent dreamland."

"Oh," he peeped.

Satisfied with my prone firing position, I turned my head slowly toward Ski. Rain streaked down the camouflaged frown on his face. He looked tense.

"Partner," I whispered. "Did I ever tell you that you're a damn good One-One?"

"No. But I kinda figured that you . . . well, you would have sent me packing by now if I wasn't doing something right. At least a fair job."

"Exceptional job. You saved my ass in Hotel Five. Did I ever buy you a beer for doing that?"

Ski blinked. "No."

"Well, remind me to do that someday," I said, turning back to peer at the vague silhouette of the slumped guard.

"Brett, you said we're firing our LAWs at the gun and not the truck, right?"

"Roger."

"Well, okay."

"Okay, what?" I whispered, turning to look at him.

"Nothing really. I just thought there might be a lot of ammo in the truck. I can't see inside it, but seems like—"

"Partner, you are abso-fucking-lutely right! That truck has to be loaded with rounds for the gun since they're obviously setting up training and emplacement."

Somewhere in the hurried planning stages I'd overlooked simple target logic.

"Partner, change ninety-nine; I want you to fire your LAWs directly into the lower rear canopy area of that—"

Suddenly, muffled, man-made thunder rent the stormy night. Then another blast sounded—Rham had detonated two charges.

I jerked my head into firing position and saw the dim profile of the guard shift upright as if startled by the noise.

Sighting center chest, I fired—the round cracked into his torso driving him backward off the seat like a fall-away target.

Dropping my rifle, I grabbed a LAW, glimpsing Ski as he shouldered one also.

I flipped the canister over my shoulder, aiming the tube point blank at the turret—my wet hand grasped the pressure trigger.

Boom! Boom! Boom! Three Claymores roared, shattering the drizzle-laced darkness. Boom! Boom! Two more sounded.

A wild chorus of human howls and yelps streamed from the hooches as a mass of kinetic silhouettes scrambled into view.

"Fire!" I cried, clamping my grasp into the rubber trigger housing. The M72 canister jolted in my grip as a white vapor trail streaked out through the wet air. A stout scent of burnt sulphur raked over me.

The ear-splitting explosion of my round impacting steel flashed bright plumes of light over the big gun—the light was quickly curtained by pale, gray smoke. Black bodies and lumped carnage spotted the radius around the gun.

"Misfire!" Ski shouted, tossing his LAW aside, grabbing another at the same time I did.

"Guns out! Blast that fucking truck!" I yelled, slamming another M72 over my shoulder.

Simultaneous triggering sent dual vapor trails hurling more HE downrange. A massive, earth-jarring explosion spewed a billowing crescendo of flames, fragments, and bodies high into the sky like a malformed, multi-colored, nuclear blast. Mammoth, secondary explosions erupted, jarring the ground beneath me and showering more debris over the village.

Ducking my head into the bent craddle of my arms, I felt airborne debris crashing over my body like solid, pelting pieces of rain.

Seconds later, I raised up, darting a look down into the smoky, cratered inferno. Mangled pieces of warped steel and smoldering bodies littered the detonation zone. The explosion of the truck had blown away half the village.

Windblown flames lofted from burning huts—nothing was moving but the thick drift of smoke as it swept a wayward path through the jagged flames.

"Ready on the Claymores," Ski shouted. "You ready to fire?"

"What for?" I answered, raising upward to my knees and scanning the vast crater for anything that resembled living matter. Nothing. Somewhere in the black distance a dog barked.

Ski raised up, muttering, "Son . . . of . . . a holy . . ." he fell silent for a second, gaping at the crater. "Where's the truck, the—the gun, the everything . . . Damn, those LAWs pack some powerful stuff!"

I grinned. "Partner, the powerful stuff was you."

"What? Me?"

"Roger, you." I answered, keeping my gaze fixed on the death zone. "It was you that reminded me about that ammo in the truck. When our rounds hit that load it was like a spark in a fireworks factory! Out-fucking-standing!" I said, reaching to pick up my grenades.

"I guess you know what this means. don't you, Brett?" Ski said, standing and brushing debris off his arms.

I stood. "What?"

Ski grinned. "I'd say it means you owe me another beer, wouldn't you say?"

"Roger, and I'm paying up just as soon as we hit sweet Thai earth at NKP. Come on, help me retrieve those Claymores."

Walking down the hill, I felt the cool rain on my neck. The monsoon was quickly extinguishing the fires.

Plodding forward, I breathed deeply, inhaling the rapturous stink of victory.

# Chapter 28

After collecting our gear and preparing to move out to the link-up point, I turned and peered toward the corpse-splotched crater zone.

"Wait here and cover me, partner," I said, glancing at Ski.

"Where you going?"

"Just be a minute. Hang tight."

I shifted my rifle sling over my neck and walked out through the sprawled bodies and twisted wreckage. The flickering remnants of dying fires danced beneath lazy spirals of pale smoke as I moved around the muddy lip of the crater.

One smoldering corpse had been penetrated with the muzzle of an AK as if the awesome velocity of the explosions had hurled a loose weapon straight into his gut.

My eyes scanned, searching for any evidence of a Havelock cap—the search was futile. It was only my visceral desire, or perhaps more—a need to find some tangible proof that the incarnate demon was shredded and lifeless.

I removed my bush hat, feeling the warm grip of some displaced pagan sense of reverence weaving through the rain.

Gazing out over the dismal wasteland, I thought of fallen comrades.

Comrades—all too often the essence of our duty amounted to being inserted up the anal canal of tyranny like a hominoid suppository; we were out-numbered, pursued, had our asses shot off, and if we were lucky enough to get out alive, we might have gained some scrap of information in the furious process that just might enhance some staff jockey's concept of how to win the fucking war.

Job gratification was as barren as the shit-stench squalor looming around me. Now I wished that the noble ghosts of fallen comrades could hover above the smoldering aftermath of this brief triumph—perhaps they'd smile and whisper, "Press on, Recon. You did good!"

# Chapter 29

Reverend Vandyke Kingston's voice quivered as I moved slowly toward the dark lean-to. "Who's—who's there—there? I can hear—hear. I—I have a gun . . . I'm warning—"

"Calm down, reverend. It's me, Yancy."

"Oh, thank God, thank God!" he chattered. "I mean that in all fervent, fervent context. Thank God!"

"There have been animals lurking about here and, I think—"

"Calm down!" I repeated, while crouching near his dim profile.

He was sitting upright. It seemed his gluteus maximus pain had been overruled by the gripping presence of fear.

He grasped my arm. "Yancy, Sergeant Yancy, I've never been more—more literally predominated by the shadow of death. I've had to shepherd—shepherd away the creatures of death!"

"Roger, I understand, reverend," I replied, grinning. "Is that a shepherd's staff in your lap or is that an instrument of the devil?" I whispered, noticing the rifle.

"Well, the Lord gave us the intelligence to form tools for our survival," he rationalized. "And what was the tremendous clamor I heard some time ago? Was that your doing, or was it—"

"My doing, reverend. You might say I was shepherding away some creatures of death, too."

"Well, thank God you're alright. I mean it! I prayed for you. You must be hungry," he said, reaching and shuffling into his pack. "I have some Fig Newtons here that you may have. Where are your men?"

"Back there," I nodded toward the rear of the shelter. "We're staying here a couple of hours 'til first light, then we'll take you and head on to another village and link up with Tuong, Rham, and the others," I answered, accepting the bag of cookies.

"Splendid! And the big sergeant, Binkowski, is he alright?"

"Roger," I said, turning to move back into the rain.

"Why must you go? I mean, where?"

"I'm going to give these to my team. These cookies you just gave me."

"Wait, please. Wait. There is something that has burdened me all night. Something I must tell you."

I yawned. "Look, reverend, I'm tired. Whatever it is can wait 'til later. Okay?"

"Sergeant, there is something you should know regarding Abraham Duell. I detest having to be adamant, but I must! I have lived with the burden of my sin all night. Please listen to me."

I was surprised to hear the pious Kingston admit to sin. At first I thought he was dramatizing a ploy, like a child that didn't want to be left alone in the dark.

"Okay, what kind of sin have you been living with?"

"The sin of—of, non-disclosure, non-truth," he answered timidly. "Mind you, I've told you the truth about Abraham, it's well, . . . it's simply that I haven't told you the entire truth. The lord has seen fit to spare me through this long and agonizing night. He has, in his divine way, given me a sign, a sign that I must convey all truth unto you."

"Fine. Okay," I agreed, feeling an irritation with myself for letting him talk me into listening. "I'll be back in a minute."

I moved outside and back to the team, giving them the food and telling them to eat and get some z's.

Moving back inside the lean-to, I told Kingston to give me his short version of the story. "Let's have it, reverend. Skip the rhetoric," I said, hearing fatigue in my voice.

I listened with strained patience while Kingston purged his sin of non-disclosure. He told me that he'd learned of a plot initiated by the Corsican opium buyers to kidnap Abraham Duell and hold him for an unconventional type of ransom—opium.

Kingston was uncertain of the exact volume of opium that the Corsicans wanted, but he was certain that it was the Corsicans who had captured Duell.

I yawned again. "That's interesting, reverend, but not possible. I've already told you that I learned from a reliable source that Duell was seen coming through Na Dao with an NVA patrol. He's headed to Hanoi, and now I'm headed to—"

"Wait! What you, or rather, your reliable source observed was a communist patrol taking Abraham to the Corsicans. That's what!"

"Look, Kingston, the NVA are fighting a war here. Why would they give a flying . . . give a hoot, or go out of their way, to help the Corsicans?"

"Two reasons! One, as I have told you, it aids their economy to eliminate Abraham's anti-opium crusade and—"

"They can do that by putting a bullet in his head," I butted in.

"Perhaps, but more paramount is reason two: money."

Kingston explained that after several failed attempts to kidnap Duell, the Corsicans finally put out a bounty on him. It was the good reverend's belief that no NVA patrol could resist the money the Corsicans were offering.

"Don't you see, sergeant? It would be utter insanity for them to kill Abraham. These soldiers are risking their lives for peanuts! And now, suddenly they are given the opportunity to do their cause honor and line their wallets with cash at the same time,'' Kingston exclaimed waving his hands. ''Don't your see?

Edging closer to his face, I cross-examined him. ''If all this is true, then why did you wait until now to tell it?''

Moments later Vandyke unfolded a story that I had no trouble believing. He said he'd felt a burning sense of professional alienation with Duell to the point of envy. He admitted that he actually enjoyed the absence of having to compete with Duell for spiritual leadership among the people.

His confessing voice wilted. ''It is the third deadly sin—jealousy. I had come to this primitive land to bring music and the word of the Lord and save souls. The Hmong have tolerated me, but it is Abe Duell they worshiped.'' The reverend sniffed, brushing tears from his eyes.

''You said something before leaving this afternoon that has echoed within me all night. You said that saving the peoples' souls wasn't worth a damn if they're dead. Isn't that what you said?''

''Roger, that's what I said.''

''Well, your words are undisputably true. Abe Duell was giving the Hmong life. He is their immediate savior . . . I well, perhaps, I am ahead of my time here and now.

''I know you must be weary, so I will tell you this, then I will let you rest, Sergeant Yancy.

''During this fearfully long and lonely night, I have seen a light, learned something that no man of God worth his pittance of salt should be without.'

''What's that?'' I asked, listening closely.

''Simply, that if one is to be a disciple of God, he must first be a disciple of truth.''

# Chapter 30

RT Texas stood with Fayden beneath a light, mid-morning drizzle saying our good-byes to Ha and the refugees of Na Dao. They'd chosen to accept Ha's guidance and journey west with him. They vowed to return for their ancestral remains when the area was secure again.

As the long string of women, children, and old men ambled slowly down the trail, I turned and saw Kingston exit the hut where we'd put Chua's papasan—he and Chua would be exfiltrating with us as soon as the weather allowed a chopper to get in to us.

Hurrying toward me with a skipping limp, Kingston grimaced, saying, "Well, Sergeant Yancy, I've done what I can for the old gentleman. He seems to have a mild case of dysentery, but he should recover soon enough with the help of good medical treatment at NKP.

"I'll be pressing on, as you say. I've decided to accompany Ha on to Xieng Khouang. They will need my help during the journey." He sighed. "I believe I'll eventually return home within a few weeks."

"Where's home?" Ski questioned, holding his hand out to Kingston.

"Ohio. Cleveland, Ohio." Vandyke answered quickly, shaking Ski's hand, then pulling it away to inspect his fingers. "You have a grip like a wrestler!"

"Thank you, sir."

"Well, good luck to you, reverend," I said, accepting his hand. "You want to carry one of these AKs along with you?"

He grinned. "No. No, thank you. I would probably be more dangerous than helpful with one of those. But then, as you have prophesied, we shouldn't encounter any problems moving west."

Kingston bounced a smiling glance along the row of Cowboys on my right, then to Fayden and Ski. His eyes stopped on me. "It may be somewhat late for me to request a favor, but—"

"Shoot, reverend."

"Well, as I have told you already, somewhere in these mountains, that crotchety, divine, old man named Abraham Duell is being held against his will by French gangsters. It is my feeling that he is somewhere up near Ban Ban," the reverend said, pointing north.

"Would you do what you can to convince the military authorities that they need to research, conduct reconnaisance, I mean, in that region? If not for me, do it for the Hmong people. They need him. . . . They need him," he said, raising his rusty eyebrows in polite emphasis.

"Roger that, reverend. I'll do what I can. I wouldn't be at all surprised if Recon Team Texas is back in this neck of the woods before long, headed north. We've been known to volunteer for some wild shi . . . missions."

"Dat rhy. We x-cep-n-al!" Tuong chimed.

"I must agree with that adjective," Kingston said, smiling and stepping back to view us. "Good-bye . . . you will all be in my prayers" He brushed a finger to his eye, then turned, hop-skipping off toward the last villagers moving down the muddy trail.

A few meters away he stopped and turned, looking back. "You know, one afternoon years ago," he shouted, "I heard a speech by President Kennedy. He said that the

Special Forces soldier was the embodiment of the term 'soldier statesman.'

"It seems strange indeed that it would take so many years, and so many miles, for me to finally learn what he meant by 'soldier statesman.'

"God bless you, gentlemen. And God bless America!"

*Author's note:* Readers' comments about this story and other *Command and Control* adventures are appreciated. Comments may be addressed to: James D. Mitchell, P.O. Box 1885, Hurst, TX 76053.